A GOOD RAM IS HARD TO FIND

Stories

by Benjamin Drevlow

Cowboy Jamboree Press
good grit lit.

Copyright © 2021 by Benjamin Drevlow.

All rights reserved. No part of this book may be reproduced or used in any manner without written permission of the copyright owner except for the use of quotations in a book review. For more information, address: cowboyjamboree@gmail.com

First Edition
ISBN: 9798487367860

www.cowboyjamboreemagazine.com

This is a work of fiction. All characters are fictional and any resemblance to persons living or deceased is coincidental.

Cover Design: Adam Van Winkle
Interior Design: Kassie Bohannon

Cowboy Jamboree Press
good grit lit.

Praise for Benjamin Drevlow and A Good Ram is Hard to Find

"These stories capture the gritty realities of traditional masculinity falling apart. The quiet intensity of stoic fathers give way to big hearted sons who take in the world unguarded. This raw, brutally honest voice had me swinging between hysterical laughter and profound awe. Each page is magnetic and I'm now a forever fan of Drevlow's writing."

~Devin Murphy, National Bestselling author of *The Boat Runner* and *Tiny Americans*

"Oh my oh my! What a gritty and poetic bunch of crazy-ass stories! Benjamin Drevlow's *A Good Ram is Hard to Find* is chock-a-block filled with lonely, troubled misfits searching for kernels of sweetness in their hardscrabble, hard-luck lives. Even while forlorn and forsaken, abused and misunderstood, each character holds tight to their good-hearted, if twisted, sense of humor. Written with guts and pathos, these wonderful tales spark and fizz with an energy that makes this book hard to put down. Find a comfy place to settle in and consume this juicy collection. I'm sure glad I did."

~Alice Kaltman, author of *Dawg Towne*

"What a mysterious and honest book. *A Good Ram is Hard to Find* captures the everyday violence of poverty, and the strange, beautiful tenacity of people living on the fringe of the working class. Together these stories capture every dark, electric detail of the least populated landscapes of modern America as we descend into what feels like the last days of late capitalism. Each story here lives and breathes and trembles like a living human."

~Chris Dennis author of *Here is What You Do*

"Benjamin Drevlow comes at the reader with a logging chain and a tattoo needle and asks, which is it going to be? Your head or your heart? *Can you smell my imagery?* He writes true grit lit like the redheaded stepchild of Flannery O'Connor and Harry Crews. Be warned, his humor has a crosscut serrated bite to it. In the title story, "A Good Ram is Hard to Find," a young man struggles to win back his ram's dignity (the ram's name, Arnold Schwarzenegger) and at the same time struggles to discover how to become a man despite the bad hand life dealt him in the family department. In "Mama's Little Helper" a manipulative mama makes her big boy and her brother-in-law complicit in the murder of her husband in a gritty, grotesque, and paradoxically hopeful story about truth you might expect from a writer like Donald Ray Pollock. Drevlow knows, like any good southern writer, that life can be heartbreaking, freakish, and ludicrous all at once. A breakthrough writer you have to know!"

~Daren Dean, author of *Far Beyond the Pale*, *The Black Harvest: A Novel of the American Civil War*, *I'll Still Be Here Long After You're Gone: Stories*, and *This Vale of Tears*

"Like the 3 Ninjas, Georgia sweet-peach Benjamin Drevlow kicks back with his latest heart-stomper, *A Good Ram is Hard to Find,* the hotly-awaited follow-up to 2019's soul-eviscerator, *Ina-Baby*. Eleven new wild and *holy-shit-*

what?? stories about pornographic puppet shows, suicidal farm boys, and drug-addicted Nazis from your childhood. Drevlow is one of the best and bravest writers we got going today, and probably the most charming middle-aged dude to sport a Mohawk since Harry Crews. I love the guy, and you will too—I'd bet my VHS copy of *3 Ninjas: High Noon at Mega Mountain* on it."

~Brian Alan Ellis, author of *Bad Poet*

"In *A Good Ram is Hard to Find*, Benjamin Drevlow unlocks the minds and desires of men on the precipice of dynamic changes. These men, struggling with the ideas and trappings of masculinity, glimmer in this new world of expression and feeling. There's grit and beauty, piss and vinegar, and something trembling under the surface of these stories, aching to be heard, swallowing pride, just for a moment of feeling. Drevlow's sentences sparkle with the unadorned voices of men who are learning to fight the silences passed on by generations of bottled-up fathers. These men don't always say the correct thing, but they're finally willing to risk letting out big feelings of olive, hate, anger, and the vulnerability of wanting to anyone else."

~Tommy Dean, author of *Special Like the People on TV*

For Arnold Schwarzenegger (RIP)

Herein

Buried Treasure	8
A Good Ram Is Hard to Find	9
The Weathermen	35
Mama's Little Helper	39
So Much Love	59
Notes on Jumping	62
Swiss	66
In Our Defense We Didn't Set Out to Make a Pornographic Puppet Show	101
How He Did It	118
Poetry	127
My Childhood PTSD as Triggered by the Following Movie Montage	135
Jonesing for Jesus	143
Work	149
How Much I Want You to Love Me	201

Benjamin Drevlow

Buried Treasure

    How you'd even react, young buck, if you knew how I ogled, like some long-lost uncle, that sliver of pale flesh running under the silver crucifix your girl said she'd never take off, how hard you've tried to anoint that sacred intersection of her chest you nuzzle in the morning shower, of course, only when you're sporting good enough wood and not too hungover. Still, my eyes can't help but connect the dots of all those freckles from too many lazy days like these under the August sun, the two of you laid out across dueling beach towels like a Cialis commercial, me plodding by with my surf socks and metal detector, this floppy hat and Hawaiian shirt, all that SPF 100 caked up and down my pasty ankles and knees, nose and cheeks, these big golden wayfarers concealing our fleeting tryst, me and your girl's tits.

A Good Ram Is Hard to Find

1.

The story of how Rusty'd gotten Arnold Schwarzenegger was the story of Rusty's old man and Rusty's two older brothers. How the boys were all supposed to have an animal, even little Rusty.

Teach them responsibility, learn 'em how to be men.

Rusty's middle brother Dickie, eight years older, having the cows and his oldest brother Ray, ten years older, having the horse and two goats, the horse's best friends, Brownie and Pumpkin, whereas Rusty—the oop-si-baby and runt of the litter—couldn't really be trusted with anything big and dangerous, how he'd gotten the sheep.

Rusty's old man taking him and his brothers to the fair state fair that year. Dickie and Ray already having their own animals to take care of, them getting free reign to check out the fancy new farming gadgets over at the tractor tent, whereas Rusty's old man leading him by his stubby little hand all the way over to the sheep barn to talk to this guy shearing this ginormous sheep.

Thor: Ram God of the Thunder. That's what the sign on his pen said in big glittery zigzaggy lettering. That and: *Returning Grand Champion State Ram*.

Big wooly Thor propped up on this shearing stand that could barely hold him, his head big as a small horse's head tethered to the stocks.

Rusty staring eye-level at Thor's mighty scrotum as Thor's owner buzzed one testicle and then the other, before heading up to the hind quarters. The whole time Thor chewing his cud peacefully, no kicking, no bahing, not even a twitch.

Or, well, at some point the mighty ram god letting his bowls open up, a mighty downpour of chocolate-covered raisins raining down over his owner's clippers and hand and some of them tumbling all the way down his wrist and into his sleeve. Thor's owner, just as stoic, going right on a shearing off all his grand champion ram's dingleberries.

Rusty so mesmerized by the whole scene, unawares of his pops resting his giant hand on the back of his neck.

What do you think, Rust?

Huh?

Sheep?

Yah, Pops.

What do you think?

About sheep?

About sheep.

They're alright, I guess.

And that's how Rusty'd gotten the Son of Thor: Ram God of Thunder aka Arnold Schwarzenegger the Terminator.

***

Arnold Schwarzenegger: Son of Thor, he'd been a late May birth. Too late to get fattened up enough to sell at the market. Too young to show at the fair.

And his mama's teats all dried up. *A goddamn bottle-feeder*. Those being the sheep guy's words, not Rusty's.

What's a guy gonna do with a goddamn bottle-feeder? the guy told Rusty's old man. He couldn't keep two rams around. Everybody knew that. What kind of flippin' nimrod didn't know that?

The gist of things best Rusty could understand.

If the old man'd ever tolerated his youngest son's questions when talking business with other men, Rusty might've pulled on his old man's shirt sleeve to ask: *But why...? Why couldn't you keep two rams around? Especially with one of the rams being Thor and the other ram being the Son of Thor?*

The question Rusty should've been asking: *Yeah, just how many sons could Thor: Ram God of Thunder sire in any given year?* And also: *Were all sons of Thor created equal?*

***

The thing about Arnold Schwarzenegger was that Rusty wasn't much for Norse mythology, but he knew comics. He also knew how Dickie and Ray'd tease the bejeesus out of him for all his superhero comics about a bunch of sissies fighting in tight tights with long flowing hair and names like Thor: God of Thunder or He-Man and the Masters of the Universe.

Dickie and Ray didn't need to read comic books to pretend how manly and tough they were, didn't need to act, they just were. Manly and tough, two chips off Rusty's old man's block. Give them cows and they'll raise cows and they'll slaughter those cows and feed the family off those cows. Give them a horse and they'll ride that horse and pull big things with that horse, things that needed to be pulled, like plows or hay wagons.

Whereas Rusty, with his one sheep, the castoff son of Thor, having to prove himself, Rusty deciding to learn by doing, doing what his brothers would do—not the farming, no—but their movies. Tough guy, manly movies like *Rambo: First Blood* or *Delta Force*, or most importantly *Terminator II: Judgement Day*, having come out the year Rusty'd gotten his ram lamb. Dickie and Ray's favorite, how they were always saying to each other: *Ah'll be bock*, which to Rusty seemed just about perfect for the name a bastard son of a Norse god. *Ah'll be bock.*

What Rusty used to tell little Arnie every time he'd get done bottle-feeding him and rough housing: *Don't you worry, little buddy. Ah'll be bock.*

How quickly Arnold'd become like a big old puppy to Rusty. Rusty could just call his name—*Arr nooold!*—and the young buck would come prancing toward him, looking for another bottle and aa head rub and just a little attention because it'd been just the two of them. Arnold: Son of Thor and Rusty: Son of Russell Sr.

How sometimes Rusty even liked to imagine himself one day writing his own comic book about it all, Arnold Schwarzenegger the cast-off ram lamb of Thor, growing up into one of the fiercest competitive rams in all Hayfield County.

A Good Ram Is Hard to Find

Ah'll be bock, Thor. And when I do, I will sit atop the throne of grand champion ram that I rightfully deserve. Something like that, but with sheep dressed up in cool manly costumes.

<u>2.</u>

My oh my, son… would you look at them hindquarters on this 'un?

First words out the mouth of the Honorable Judge Nygard, nineteen years and running Head Sheeping Judge of Hayfield County.

Little Rusty eight years old and done up in his Sunday best, down on one knee out the in the middle of the show ring with Arnold.

Oh gosh, oh golly, ladies and gentlemen. Judge Nygard declaring to the entire sheep barn. Shoo… this young feller might be the finest physical specimen I seen in a couple summers.

Rusty looking around to see the whole show ring silent and listening. The other kids with their smaller, less imposing rams having stand there and to listen to it. Those kids' parents watching outside the ring.

Rusty looking this way and that, looking for the looks on his old man and Dickie and Ray, not finding them anyway, but imagining their looks just the same, the three of them bearing witness to this sheep judge declaring for all the world what a fierce combatant Arnold Schwarzenegger had already grown into. And in just one year.

Judge Nygard saying for real: Mm-mm-mm, would you look at those rear flanks. Judge running his hands all along the sharp edges of Arnold's massive frame. Look at muscling running up from the shoulder to middle neck. Look at those loins, those hindquarters.

Oh my, ladies and gentlemen.

Rusty so caught up in basking, looking for the beaming eyes of his old man, and maybe the slightly less beaming eyes of his big brothers. Rusty so caught up and taking all this in and never picking up on the quiet little shift in Judge Nygard's north country lilt.

Oh gosh, oh goll-lee, ladies in gentlemen... Judge shaking his head, clicking his tongue tsk, tsk, tsk.

...which is why I was just so disappointed for this young man... Judge having bent down to one knee just like Rusty, but from behind Arnold's tremendous rear flanks.

Judge stopping mid-sentence, to add to all the drama, to get another feel for things, as if not really believing what all he'd been seeing and feeling.

Arnold posing stoically this whole time. A regular chip off the old God of Thunder block. No jumping, no kicking, not even a twitch as the judge groped him this way and that in front of a crowd of people.

The judge giving Rusty a half-smile, the half-smile you give a kid when you pick him last in the peewee lottery. Judge going back to his whole tongue-clicking, head-shaking routine before whispering oh gosh, oh golly, son and patting both Rusty and Arnold on their rumps.

You see here, ladies and gentlemen. Judge Nygard squatting there behind Arnold like a catcher now. For a moment, Rusty could not see what all the judge was seeing, what all the show ring was now seeing, Rusty being blocked out by the giant physical specimen that was Arnold.

What Rusty'd been missing: Arnold's itty-bitty scrotum palmed in his hand, Judge shaking it gently like he was about to play a game of cornhole with it.

Ladies and gentlemen, this here young fella might be built like a Johnny. But when you get up under the hood there... So sad, how this strapping young buck's working with nothing but an old two stroker weedwhip.

Some sniggers and guffaws erupting right then from all around the ring. Even a couple other rams in the ring let out a big old bleat at Rusty and Arnold's expense. And now half the sheep back in the barn were bleating their asses off too.

The judge still running his mouth. *Oh gosh oh golly, son, I'm sorry to tell ya that this here ram ain't never gonna be nothing but eye candy for ya. He sure ain't gon' sire you no champion stock, son. Not with BBs like these for baby ammunition.*

The whole crowd hooting with laughter, the whole sheep barn erupting right along with them, all them dicks yucking it up and Rusty and Arnold's expense.

I'll give the young buck this, though. Bless his big ram heart. Look at that stance on him. He sho' is proud of what little he do have, ain't he, ladies and gentlemen?

All this insult to injury as he motioned for Rusty and Arnold to get the second-place ribbon for their yearling rams.

And afterward, how Rusty looked and looked, but there was no phone number listed on the front or back of that ribbon. Nothing listed about who he should talk to about getting his ram's dignity back.

<u>3.</u>

You might could call it the story of the little engine that could, what Rusty sometimes imagined telling young sheep-showers years down the road. Arnold having proven that judge wrong and that sheep guy who sold him off wrong and probably his old man Thor wrong too. In fact, both their old men wrong.

Inspire those future sheepers but also teach them an important life lesson about persistence in the face of doubt. Imagine how legendary the legend of Arnold Schwarzenegger would grow and grow with each grand-champion progeny he'd sire.

In Rusty's mind anyway.

Sure, Arnold never growing himself a decent pair of gonads, pretty much topping out at two marbles strung up in a coin purse. But then never letting that get in his way or slow him down in his pursuits of spreading his seed.

Yet, within a week of Rusty and his old man strapping that red humping chalk right down there to mark where the magic happened, the hindquarters of all of Rusty's ewes having been red as roses ever since. Each one birthing a pair of twins that winter.

And same thing every summer. The big strapping buck sowing his wild oats and deploying payload after payload of those little sperms like heat-seeking torpedoes in search of that mighty ovum.

Arnold Schwarzenegger didn't just inseminate. He reaped. He sowed. He fertilized!

Like clockwork every spring, Arnie'd sire at least two, three ram lambs in his own likeness. Long, thick, wide, and rangy, pretty much the whole package you could ask for in a ram. Everything except that one little part of the package where they all, always fell a little short.

The legend of Arnold quickly being recast as the curse of Thor's Bastard Son. The vicious cycle of ram siring—small package begets small package and so on and so forth.

***

A late May birth should've been the first omen of change.

Not twins or triplets, this time. One single ram lamb who just so happened to have a frame on him like a newborn horse. Frame that looked to rival even his mighty father.

Rusty, twelve years old now and both his brothers away at school. His old man older and ornerier with every year, propping the young buck on his knee like a deranged Santa. Rusty down on his knees and leaning in, ready to bite down on the epididymis of one more sad little gonad, one more shriveled little teste.

Rusty now learned in the castration methods of old, the way his old man had learned to castrate sheep and his old man before him. To get even the littlest taste of what it meant to remove a testicle from another animal.

How many times Rusty'd vomited while learning his craft and trade the way his old man had passed down to him. Rusty literally biting off more than he could chew.

Not a pretty picture, but still, somehow in all that, Rusty managing to keep his wits about him, to hold in his vomit with one hand, all the while he's groping with the other. Grabbing and grabbing some more to get around to the circumference of all that. All that nutty goodness up there, Rusty couldn't seem to get a grip on it all, couldn't get his mind around it, let alone his fingers.

And Rusty's old man getting in there too, groped them up a bit, massaging them from side to side and pulling a little at the scrotum. The old man letting out a deep sigh and scratching at the stubble on this chin a bit and even groaned a little, but what he ends up telling Rusty is Well, everything up in there feels healthy to me.

The old man even shooting Rusty a slightest of smirks on that one. Taking his hand off that ram lamb's nuts and placing it on Rusty's shoulders.

Nope, Rust. This 'un here, he looks like he might be the full package.

The total package?

The old man reaching over with his big mitt of a hand to grab Rusty around the nape of his neck. And then out of everything possible, a smile. A real smile for maybe the first time in Rusty's whole life.

Well, son, don't go putting old Arnold out to pasture just yet, but…

<u>4.</u>

It almost broke Rusty's heart to have to break it up. But it was time.

Arnold Sr., five years old now but prancing about the corral like a yearling. Senior and Junior rubbing up against each other and knocking heads as if they were giving each other high-fives. The two of them attached at the shoulders circling this way and that way around the corral, first Junior trying to push his weight around, then of course Arnold Sr. returning the favor, but with a tender playfulness, a show of love between father and son.

Two hours to fair registration, Rusty's first year of leaving the old guy home.

You gonna have to hold down the fort, old man, Rusty whispering in the senior ram's ears, taking time out from fair preparations to give the big guy one last good head-scratching.

No muss, no fuss this year. You don't need some pompous judge getting up in your business. Telling you ain't ram enough to raise a championship flock.

No, buddy, you've done put in all your work. Put in your time. Time's come to let Junior here do your talking for you, eh?

Rusty in middle of the pasture, having turned his back on Arnold to go corral up Junior. Rusty almost tearing up thinking about all him and Arnold having been through and now all coming to fruition with Junior.

Junior? Rusty calling out, whistling. Eh Junior, it's your time, young buck. Time to make your daddy proud.

The first jolt up Rusty's spine, like to've backed into the electric fence again.

The second one, what turned him around in his tracks. Those big dark eyes of Arnold's staring Rusty down. His frame dwarfing Rusty and the morning sun as he reared back on his hind legs.

Whoa boy, Rusty starting to say, but only getting to *whu*—Arnold Schwarzenegger: Son of Thor dropping the hammer on Rusty the way he was born to.

Like straight out of the original comic book—*Pow!* Rusty's little dialogue bubble reading: *Harumpf!* Or maybe: *Ugh...!*

Except for the comic writer keeping things PG and kid-friendly, probably it'd be Thor's hammer straight to some costumed baddie's gut or head or solar plexus.

Rusty took it straight to the nads.

Everything down there on Rusty suddenly pulsing, throbbing, and radiating an ache at once sharp and dull. Seemingly pleading with a voice of its own, *Why? Why? Why? What've I ever done to deserve this?*

Arnold no longer rearing back or pawing at the ground, Rusty listening to the short snotty breathing only inches away from where he lay curled up in mud and manure.

At some point Rusty's old man hollering from the truck, asking why Junior wasn't loaded up yet. You had one job, Rust...

It must've been quite a sight. Rusty crawling on his hands and knees as that old ram sniffed and snorted and started to rub up against Rusty's throbbing body.

The old man clicking his tongue and cocking his head as he reached out to help Rusty up. How many goddamn times I gotta tell you, boy? These ain't your puppies. These are big strong animals that'll put a hurtin' on you in hurry.

Yes sir, Rusty saying. No sir. I know, sir.

How many times Rusty'd said those same words on the way to the fair.

Boy, you ain't a kid no more, his old man kept saying.

This ain't no play time out there on the farm.

Yes, sir. No sir. I know, sir.

This is just the tip of the iceberg, his pops saying. You gonna have to make a decision, you know? Can't have two old bucks runnin' around the same pasture. Competing against each other. It's only a matter of time 'til one of them starts fixin' to show the other one who's in charge.

Yes, sir. No sir. I know sir.

All Rusty could to get out much more than a whisper and a groan without his voice cracking and his eyes starting to water again.

<u>5.</u>

But the look on Judge Nygard's face that year almost making up for everything else. A perfect human O. His meaty hands up underneath Junior's rear flanks.

The man borderline speechless. So tickled by what he's found up under Junior's hood to say my oh my oh mines… Whole time smirking up at Rusty and then looking up toward all the people gathered around the show ring, then back at his hands up there in Junior's parts and then back up at Rusty.

Well, well, well, he kept on saying. And then, my oh my oh my….

Eventually, Judge Nygard managing to gather himself enough to get back to his feet, taking one last survey of the field before placing.

Rusty almost missing it the first time, judge calling his name. Contestant number seven? Judge clearing his throat, pointing, saying again, Contestant number seven?

Then: You got water in your ears, son? Pull your big feller right on up here next to me.

No other rams out there in front of Rusty and Junior. Rest of them still waiting for their names to be called, waiting to watch Rusty lead big Junior in front of all them, show them what a pair of champions looked like.

Do a victory lap. Walk the catwalk. Strut their stuff. Bask in their glory.

Little crusty Rusty, half grown up. Smirk on him like the cat that ate the canary, feathers and all. Even Junior letting out a big old bah! as declaration of his ascension to the crown.

All them peoples standing around the ring smiling and clapping as Judge Nygard's announcing Rusty's name and Junior's name—Arnold Aloysius Schwarzenegger II—Hayfield County's Grand Champion ram, 1993.

Grand Champeen, saying it like that and handing Rusty that big frilly purple grand ribbon and that big shiny gold ram standing atop that trophy.

All those beaming faces save for the most important one.

***

Rusty's crowning achievement as a sheeping man and where'd his old man been to celebrate it?

The old man ducking out early to take down the show pens, load up the other sheep, get a head start home to do chores for the rest of the animals.

Nope, no pats on the back for Rusty. No knowing head nods, no hand on the shoulders. No *Always knew I'd make a man out of you, son*. None of that.

All business as usual, Rusty's old man. Whole ride home from the fair that night and his old man going on about the future. Making tough decisions.

While Rusty'd been letting his ego get all shined up in that show ring, his old man, he'd been in the back talking to some guy looking to break in a new ram for his flock.

Made us quite a respectable offer according to Rusty's old man. Considering pretty as he is to look at, we don't have much use for Junior back home, eh?

Eh, what? Rusty forgetting himself. then gulping, clearing his throat, fingering the frilly purple ribbon in one hand, the engraved trophy in the other.

What what?

Nothin', Pops. Rusty clearing this throat one more time, composing himself. I mean yes sir, Rusty correcting himself.

Rusty wanting more than anything to ask what a respectable offer on a grand champion ram amounted to. Wanting to ask if his old man had already signed the papers or whatever it was when one man sold his prize ram to another man? Wanting most of all to ask what kinda no sense it made why they wouldn't keep Junior the grand champion and sell off old Arnold what with all his second-place shortcomings.

All these questions and at some point, Rusty snapped a little inside. Couldn't help himself. Do we have to get rid of him as before we get back, Pops?

The whine in Rusty's voice, the look on his old man's face, but Rusty doubling down anyway: Can we take him home for day at least, Pops? Let him say goodbye to his daddy?

<u>6.</u>

Rusty not bothering to bring out the loading chutes to direct the sheep back into their barn. Let all the sheep have a big old sniffing reunion after four days away at the fair.

A beautiful thing, watching them all join each other back into the fold like that—no petty jealousies, no hard feelings, just a little sniffing and snorting and rubbing up against each other and pretty quick they were all back to eating some hay and chewing the cud in one big happy family again.

He'd get to penning up Junior in a minute or two. For now, let Junior have his triumphant homecoming. Let him prance around a bit, get his ya-ya's out. Let the young buck and his old man have one last romp around the place, say their proper goodbyes.

And so there they were off in the corner of the barn already greeting each other. Junior giddy and jumping in circles around the old guy. Junior getting so excited at one point he ends up headbutting Arnold right on the rumpus.

Rusty letting out a little giggle at first, the giggle coming out embarrassingly close to *tee-hee-hee*. Well turnabout's fair play, Rusty thinking to himself. And: How you like it when the shoe's on the other hoof, you ornery old bastard?

Arnold then returning the favor with a bit more oomph to it. Maybe a hundred, hundred fifty more pounds behind it. But then, wouldn't be old Arnie if he didn't show the young buck who's boss.

Rusty telling himself, And that's what your old man's there for, To push your buttons a bit. Make it hard on you. Make you earn your respect.

Rusty still leaning with his arms up over the front gate, stuck in his post-championship glow, his shiny sheep trophy in one hand, frilly purple ribbon in the other. Everything slowing down for a moment, first in a good slow down, then in a bad.

Junior backing up a few steps. Arnold standing his ground, snorting and pawing at the straw.

Junior rearing back and then Arnold. Both rams balancing on their back hooves for what seems like minutes. Then that thunk of skull against skull. Junior's groan, the sucking then wheezing coming up from deep in his throat. Junior stumbling backward. Sniffing a bit, shaking his head, once and then again.

Arnold already back on his hind legs, already dropping the hammer a second time before Junior can shake off the first one. Junior woozy and punch-drunk, dropping to his knees, stumbling again, then catching himself before gathering himself one last time.

Rusty just standing there, eyes wide and mouth agape at the grandeur of it all. Father pitted against Son, Son against Father.

Arnold Schwarzenegger: Son of Arnold Schwarzenegger. Arnold Schwarzenegger: Son of Thor.

The third one, a softer crack this time, like smashing a rotten cantaloupe with the concrete sidewalk. Those horrible garbled, bleating wails coming from Junior. Junior down on his side, flailing and flopping around, to protect himself, to right himself, to keep time with his scrambled brains. And Arnold showing no mercy, dropping headbutts one after another.

And Rusty useless to all the world, crying *Whoa...!* And *Stop...!* And *Stooooooppp!* And everything eventually coming to a stop. Eventually.

7.

The carnage over in how long, too long, not long enough, no more bleating, no more wheezing, groaning, no more head butting, only the small puddle of blood pooling onto the straw around Junior's muzzle.

What'd you do, you bastard? Rusty shouting at Arnold. *Why? Why? Why? What did I ever do to deserve this?* Rusty kicking himself—then kicking Arnold. In the head, in the ribs, the loins, the back.

Arnold flinching less and less with each kick. Not even bothering to move out of the way. The old ram absorbing each kick with an almost inaudible grunt and sometimes more of a sigh.

As if the old ram was almost embarrassed for Rusty and his desperate pathetic kicks of a boy—not a man. So Rusty resorting to what he had to, Rusty punching now too in between the kicking, and with even less success. His knuckles cracking and bending with each ridge of the ram's cushioned skeleton.

He was sobbing by then, yelling at the old ram to be hurt somehow, to be wounded too. Rusty's old man finding him back at the barn, shouting at him That make you feel like a real man? Taking out your shame on a dumb animal who ain't done nothing to you other than be the animal he is?

Rusty ignoring him for the first time in his life, Rusty going right on kicking and punching and yelling *Why, why, why…?* his voice cracking more with each syllable until the old man finally pulls his youngest and most useless son of the ram.

Big old Arnold snorting and eventually turning up his nose at Rusty, trotting away, back with the rest of his flock, his flock that he wasn't ready to give up quite yet.

What were you thinking? The old man kneeling between Rusty and the still body of the young ram lying prone in the corner of the barn. Examining the blood no longer running from its nostrils, its nose no longer snorting or huffing or breathing at all. Its mouth no longer bleating or calling out for Rusty to come save it.

What'd Rusty been thinking? He hadn't been. Had never been. Not truly. Ever. Thinking. At all. And this all, what he'd done to his grand champion ram. What he'd done himself. Again. Like always.

<u>8.</u>

The old man telling Rusty over and over how crying never helped nobody.

What was important was that Rusty finally learned something from his mistakes. That Rusty needed to learn to listen when his pops was telling him what to pay attention to. That Rusty start taking responsibility for his actions and inactions.

That if Rusty'd've just listened for once to what his old man'd been trying to tell him, none of this all wouldn't've happened.

Are you listening to me, Rusty?

Rusty having retrieved the wheelbarrow and shovels as the old man'd instructed.

No sir... I mean yes sir... I mean... Rusty couldn't help but sniffle one more time as he bent down to pick up Junior's legs. They were still warm, not stiff yet. Limp.

Rusty trying to hoist the dead ram's front legs into the wheelbarrow by himself, trying and failing, only to watch Junior's muzzle flop back down in the dirt and manure once and twice and again.

Rusty's old man bound and determined to make Rusty do this whole damn thing by himself. Some sort of lesson here Rusty supposed to be learning, the major them: crying never helping nobody.

The man having no goddamn heart, Rusty wanting to tell him. *You got no goddamn heart!* Shout that as low as he could muster. What kind of father refusing to help his own kid pick up his own dead ram? What it even mattered if his kid'd been responsible for getting that ram killed in the first place? *What kind of man?*

No, no, no, the old man saying. Bend with the knees. Not with the back. No, no, no, squat down low wide when you grab him. Like you got weight of the whole world on your shoulders, son.

The whole damn world, Junior's legs hugged to Rusty's chest hard as he'd ever hugged anything in his life, how he'd managed to hoist up Junior's front end this time, just high enough to clear the top of the wheelbarrow.

All right now, we're just gonna give him a little swing, you hear me?

Rusty not saying anything, not yes sir, not I know sir, not even *mm-hmm*.

Just to get up and over. We don't want to tip 'er.

Just like you're rocking him to sleep, the old man almost whispering for some reason. One.... Two... Rusty losing his grip with each number, letting go on three.

The wheelbarrow rocking this way and that, like a cradle, it was all too much, Rusty thinking to himself. *Rock-a-by-baby... And the cradle will fall...* With Junior's stiffening corpse underneath it.

The old man letting out quite possibly the longest saddest sigh Rusty having ever heard from him. His big old ham hock of a hand rubbing his forehead, his half-smashed thumb scratching slightly at his hairline.

Well don't just stand there, Rusty. Go tip it back over.

9.

Of all the things the old man having said that night, the worst being that it was too late. Too late to fix anything. Too dark to dig a proper hole.

Rusty having mostly forgotten his deference to his old man by then. Rusty both begging and declaring his intentions to stay out there all night and dig it by himself if he had to.

Just let me do it then, Pops. There's the moon, I can see fine. Just let me do it, I need to do this.

The old man as always adamant about not doing anything the Rusty way. Too dark, the old man saying, then saying again. It's too dark out, Rusty. Just leave the body locked up in the shed so coyotes don't get at it.

Please, Rusty had said finally. Pops? I just want to get it all over with.

Let it go, Rusty, the old man mumbling as he headed back to the house. You can wait 'til morning.

No, no, perhaps for the first time in his life Rusty could not let it go, could not take the old man's advice. Rusty wasn't gonna let Junior spend the night in the shed.

No, Rusty had other intentions. Rusty was gonna sneak out after bed and dig himself a big old hole out in the field behind the barn. Rusty was gonna dump Junior's dead body in that hole and then fill it all back in nice, as if nothing had ever happened. Stomp all that down, do a rain dance all over the top of Junior's fresh grave. Do all that by himself. Maybe even sleep out there under the moonlight. Keep Junior company in his sad, lonely transition to the next life.

Or something like that, Rusty telling himself. Try at least. Do that much. Try.

Rusty out there at the barn way past his bedtime. Leaning his shovel up against the side of the barn, opening the gate all slowly so the hinges wouldn't creek. Creeping around the sheep barn in the dark with only a flashlight and the narrowest of moon sneaking through the windows.

Rusty still waiting for his night vision to kick in when he ran smack dab into him. Arnold sticking his head up between Rusty's legs like the big puppy he used to be, just a big wooly puppy with no mother and no father and only Rusty out to nurse him another bottle for formula.

Five years since Rusty'd bottle fed him twice a day, the fully-body rubs, the head-scratchers, handfuls of treats. Five years of Rusty heading out to feed the sheep only to find Arnold waiting for him, waiting for another scratch, rub, another handful of treats. Maybe a walk out to the good grass back behind the barn, the good old days.

How many big, beautiful lambs Arnold'd sired. How many big, beautiful lambs Rusty'd birthed and castrated and taken to the fair only to come up short where it mattered most. Then sold for meat.

Five years and Rusty once again succumbing to that persuasive muzzle of Arnold's, Rusty scratching his head and then neck and own down his back. Rusty half-nodding off, half-dreaming, his foggy thoughts of Junior and lost possibilities and karma and maybe his old man had been right all along. About everything.

What a stupid idea this all was, all of it. raising sheep, showing sheep, Rusty trying to make a man of himself, make his old man proud, and now Rusty directly disobeying him. Sneaking out in the middle of the night to try to bury a dead sheep just so he could prove his old man wrong. Rusty rubbing that big wooly noggin and thinking about how hard and soft things could be at the same time.

A Good Ram Is Hard to Find

Hard and soft. It was a weird thing, but suddenly Rusty thinking he'd finally figured it all out, what his old man had been trying to teach him all this time.

Rusty's thoughts falling back on the dead ram lying in the wheelbarrow off in the shed. Stiffening, softening, maybe starting to stink, what did Rusty know of dead sheep. Junior being his first.

Everything making sense now. Life and death and fathers and sons, men and boys, and sheep.

All so sad and beautiful and inevitable at the same time. Rusty's eyes welling up as he leaned down to rub heads with old Arnold. Scratch him up under the chin. How many scratches Rusty'd scratched old Arnold over the years, no limit to the amount of scratching Arnold could take, no limit to the amount of scratching that Rusty owed the old guy. Especially now. In lieu of everything.

He sniffled one last little sniffle and thinking that last thing that made him smile almost. Crying.

The way crying never accomplished anything. Now does it, old man? Rusty talking to Arnold at the same time as his old man.

Rusty asking the old ram, Crying never accomplished anything, now does it? Rusty shouting now, inches from Arnold's face. Now does it?

Rusty imagining the story he'd tell his own boy one day. About crying and sheep and testicular fortitude. How Rusty'd tell them to whole heartwarming story of Arnold Schwarzenegger, Sr. Bastard Son of Thor, Ram God of Thunder.

Arnold the Underdog. The little engine that could. Arnold the Terminator. *Ah'll be bock*, Rusty telling his boys with a wink. Making a joke about a movie they'd never seen or care to see.

Or maybe he'd spare them all the sentimentalizing. Maybe he'd be the ornery patriarch the way his old man'd raised him. Tell them the true story of Arnold, sans embellishments, emphasis on all the cut and dry mistakes Rusty'd made along the way.

One hell of a ram, though, Rusty whispering to himself, having picked his shovel back up. Rusty gripping the handle firm with both hands, but not too firm either. The way his old man'd once taught him to hit a baseball.

Deep breaths in and out, Rusty taking a step back, measuring himself, then stepping back into the batters' box, his eyes wide but focused, everything in focus for once. Nothing in his way, nothing distracting him from what needed to be done.

The Weathermen

It's not even the end of March in Mankato and already it's eighty degrees out. *Global warming's coming to skewer us all!* Or at least that's what a couple of trust-fund tree-huggers are hollering about outside the student union.

The world has a fever, they keep saying into their portable microphone. A fever! They shout it with enough speaker static to be mistaken for real passion. Loud enough anyway to convince a couple of American Eagle hippies with hard-ons for hairy chicks to whistle and applaud while the rest of the students glare and whisper. Unless we quit shaving our armpits, quit wearing deodorant, start growing out our white kid dreadlocks, the planet is going to sweat us out on a stinky gym towel and toss us in the stinky hamper that is oblivion.

But I think I can go ahead and speak for all those Young Republicans in the house when I say, I'll take all the global warming I can get. It'll probably snow tomorrow or worse in this land of Minnesnowda where weathermen have to weatherproof their hair, don weather appropriate apparel, and load up on lithium before letting their manic depression step in front of that green screen weather every night. The green screen where they superimpose our snow, sleet, and blizzards for us so—just in case we don't know what a wind-chill factor of negative fifty feels like—at least we can imagine what it looks like. Yeah, Minnesota, where crop farmers drink too much corn whiskey and get fed up with Mother Nature's cock teasing, then head out to statutorily rape the soil with plows three months early. Where we tune to the weather channel just hoping for global warming. When's our turn? we ask. When's the warm front coming our way?

It's too late anyway. Me and the rest of the world at large. My rent check having already bounced at the campus credit union. *Too bad, so sad. That'll be twenty-nine-ninety-nine courtesy pay for your trouble.* And here I am waiting for a couple of daddy's girls in overalls to tell me how global warming is responsible for robbing me of my twenty-nine-ninety-nine, or how saving the world's gonna pay my rent.

Out in the courtyard the co-eds are on the grass sunning in their short-shorts and tank tops. Bra-less and letting their shoulder straps slip off their shoulders just to prove it to you. And the frat boys, topless and tossing the football around. Baring their finely-honed and bench-press-sculpted man boobs. Showing off those taut little pencil-eraser nipples for all us fatty-hairy-nippled, non-frat guys to admire. Those knock-off Native American tattoos and painted-on Paris Hilton tans. Who wouldn't want to get drunk off too many Mike's Hards and get rabbit-mounted by one of these studs?

And there's me—the crotch of my multi-colored chili-pepper pants ripped open and reeking of swamp-ass and waffles. My mohawk spiked high and tight, gelled prickly with maple syrup and grill sweat. Walking around a campus I no longer have any right to be on. A school bank account I should have closed a year ago. A year ago, when

A Good Ram Is Hard to Find

I was a peon grad student and a TA. A year ago when I had a reason to ogle undergrads. A year ago when I taught them the five-paragraph essay in trade.

And today it's March and eighty degrees out. I'm an egg cook and a dirty, crotch-smelling degenerate, so I'm on my way back to my apartment before the warm breeze catches my taint stink and some high strung bra-less former comp student calls the campus police to have me removed for acting pervy. And when I get home, Stan, the five-o-clock weather guy, winks at me and tells me to enjoy it while it lasts. And I'll be damned if he doesn't start spouting off on Horace and seizing the day. Carpe diem, he tells me, for tomorrow expect freezing rain in the early morning, sleet in the afternoon, and big puffy coats for the rest of eternity. The extended forecast: shoulder straps going back up shoulders, bras coming back out, and the little co-eds heading back to their fifth-floor dorm rooms, their high-rider thongs and halter-tops headed back to their Friday Night Clubbing drawer. And then Stan the weatherman grabs a green-screen Corona out of his green-screen beach cooler, pulls out a green-screen beach chair and grabs a little green-screen R&R in his green-screen sunshine glory.

Me? I'm with these pretty little tree-huggers. The entire damn world is suffering from something, and I'm tired of battling the fatigue and nausea of this heat stroke. Miss Mother Nature, milady, my misery it cometh, you taketh away. Hell hath no fury. Scorned, may you scorch us all. Fry our brains right out here on the pavement like those drugs we took were supposed to do. Just make mine over easy with a little extra run. I'd hate for the last taste in my mouth to be chalky and mushy and completely devoid of anything wet or salty or savory whatsoever.

Mama's Little Helper

Mama says there's no way they'll believe her now. Daddy's stretched out over the back of the couch, face hanging slack jawed upside down, the hole in his head still dripping little bits of dark red on the larger puddle streaming off the edge of the leather seat cushion. I'm no detective, but I think the reason Mama says they'll never believe her, it's because of the other bigger hole in his chest bleeding down the back of the couch.

An hour earlier, I'd've told you that shotguns were the safest guns you can own. Shotguns were for hunting pheasants and scaring off raccoons. Shotguns were for father-son bonding time.

An hour earlier, my daddy'd've said the same thing, but then he'd've added what he told me the first time he showed me how to shoot one. Boy, any man, if he's a real man, he's gotta learn how to use one of these to protect himself, his family, and his hard-earned possessions.

I'm sitting at the kitchen table and staring blankly over into the living room at how wrong Daddy turned out to be when I ask Mama why she thinks Daddy'd tried to kill himself?

She takes a long drag off her cig, coughs twice into her fist, and tells me in that pack-a-day voice of hers, Baby, it's not polite to disparage the recently dead, but you ain't a kid no more and you need to know your daddy was a sick, sick man.

Sick from what?

She drops her cigarette butt into an empty Bud and tells me he was sick all over. Cancer? I ask.

She gets up and comes around the table toward me. She rests one hand on my shoulders, the other holding up my chin so I have to strain to look back into her eyes. She says, Baby, we don't have time for goddamn twenty questions tonight. Tonight, your mama needs you to grow your little sissy ass up and act like a man.

When she tells me what she needs me to be a man for her, I say, What? at first like I don't understand her. When she tells me again more slowly, I ask her if she's drunk?

She slaps me across the face, not hard, just hard enough to get my attention. Me and my ADHD, Mama says sometimes I just need a little helping hand to keep my head on straight.

She keeps hold of my chin with one hand, her other hand, her slapping hand she's holding out flat in front of me, fingers spread and unshaking. She takes a long exhale, blows her cigarette breath in my face. Baby, she says, your mama might be stone cold sober for the time since the day she squeezed you out into this ugly world.

Then she asks again if I'm ready to step up and be a man.

I ask her if she's messing with me, if this is some sort of test to see—.

She slaps me again, harder this time. Says, It *is* a test, baby. It's a test of how much you love your mama. And so far, you ain't off to a good start.

I ask Ma, Didn't you always raise me to respect women? Didn't you always tell me to learn from Daddy's mistakes?

I can hear the little kid in me whining when I say it, and I feel my face turning red, but I blurt it out anyway: Mama, I don't wanna punch you. I say, Can't we just call the cops? Tell them it was all an accident like you said? He was trying to kill himself. You were trying to wrestle the gun away. Mama, it's like you were the hero. Kinda.

Robbie, she says and wraps her arms around me from behind. Bless your big damn heart, that simple-ass mind of yours never ceases to amaze me. She whispers it in my ear all raspy and choked up, then kisses my cheek. Your daddy, God rest his soul, you know same as I do, he was a wife-beating worthless sack of shit and now he's dead, good riddance, there's no bringing him back. But do you want the cops to come take your mama from you too?

Please believe, I love my mama with all my heart, I do. And I know that without her love and somewhat opinionated forgiveness, I may've never survived my own childhood and it's because of that love, that debt I can never truly pay back, that I stand up from the table, turn, sniffle one more time, and smack her square in the face, though not as hard as I could've if it'd been Daddy wanting me to smack him.

I don't break her nose or jaw that I can see. I don't cut open her cheek or eyebrow. Actually I can't make out any serious damage other than a slight general redness, and I'm feeling pretty good about that but kind of cowardly too. Then I see the look she's giving me, blinking and feeling her cheek, finding no blood, nothing broken. Her eyes cut straight to the bone of me. She cracks her neck, says, Haven't I always loved you, Robbie?

And I say, Yes, Mama.

And then she says, Haven't I always taken care of you and protected you, sacrificed myself to save you from Daddy's nastiness?

Yes, Mama.

Haven't I?

Yes, ma'am.

And now here we are when I need you the most, my fate hanging in the air, and here I am starting to think maybe your daddy was right about you all along.

What's that, Mama?

Baby, you are twenty-two goddamn years old and you still here sucking on your Mama's tit.

It's the guilt doing the talking, I tell myself. The trauma, the shock of it all saying these ugly things to me. I imagine it's same thing seems to finally make her snap on me. Slapping herself across the face and shaking her head at me, her hair whipping this way and that like shaking out a dirty mop. She starts balling up her fists, pounding on her thighs, marching in place. Eventually she gets to breathing too hard, starts wheezing, coughing, hacking up phlegm from deep down in her lungs. She takes deep slow breaths to catch herself, then stops, looks back up at me, and smiles that yellow toothed smile. Out of nowhere, she peals her shirt off right in front of me. She ain't got no bra on or nothing.

Get yourself a good look, boy, she says. Because you done suckled off these tits for the last time. I'm shriveled up. You gone and sucked me dry. Mama's got no more milk left to give you, baby boy.

She turns sideways to me, grabs herself a handful of flesh and grabs me by the wrist to show me what she wants. These jagged purple veins zig-zagging through an old yellowed bruise from where Daddy used to catch her with the rabbit punches, places outsiders wouldn't be able to see any signs of abuse.

This is for your mama's livelihood we're talking about here, she says. The rest of her life, it's in your hands now, Robbie. A few old faded bruises ain't gonna cut it. You gonna have to break a rib if we're gonna have half a chance in hell of anybody believing us.

I look at Mama's leathery old love handle and think of Rocky in *Rocky IV*. Ivan Drago having already killed Rocky's best friend and all those commie Russians taunting him. I think of the crowd slowly turning in Rocky's favor as the music starts to play. I think of chopping the big guy down to size with all them body blows. I think of that other earlier Rocky, old Mickey holding the heavy bag for him and shouting harder, harder. I think of all those beef carcasses hanging in the meatpacking plant, the blood all over his fists as he hits them and hits them. I feel that crunch of mama's ribs under my fist and think I'm gonna be sick.

***

Uncle Leland, daddy's brother, ends up being the first one on the scene. He's a volunteer firefighter and EMT. He's got his medical kit. He's dressed in that navy-blue uniform. All business.

He doesn't knock. He doesn't say a word. He steps through the sliding doors off the back patio and strides in like he's already been briefed on the situation. He doesn't look at me or Mama. We're back at the kitchen table, Mama chain smoking and taking hits off a fifth of Beam, me with my head in my hands, both of us watching silently as he heads straight for his dead brother. I glance at the front door and then again the back. I can't see or hear any signs of other guys he works with coming to assist him.

He takes a good long look at his brother stretched out over the couch and then back at us. He doesn't so much as sniffle or wipe away a tear. Jesus Christ, he says. What the hell you go and do that for?

He wouldn't let go of the gun for the life of me, Mama half-whines, half-shouts. You gotta believe me, Lee. He was fixin' to take me with him. Mama's stood up now, stepped between me and Uncle Leland standing over his dead brother.

Uncle Lee mutters something, shakes his head, and goes back to work. He snaps on his latex gloves and examines the body. He pokes and prods in the nasty places, he works the elbow and knee joints like he's giving a physical. He doesn't bother checking for a pulse.

How long? he says.

Mama doesn't answer. She walks over arms out for a big embrace. Oh Lee, oh Lee, it was terrible, just terrible. She's acting almost teary-eyed and weak in a way she never acted around Daddy.

But with Uncle Leland now, she's acting frail and trying to drape herself on him to hold her up. You should've seen the look in his eyes, Lee, she's saying. He was gonna do it, by God, he was gonna take me with him. Look what he did to his own damn dog.

Mr. T's lying on his side with a disturbing half-smile, soaking into a puddle of his own blood at Daddy's dangling bare feet. She points down at Mr. T the way she's always pointed at Mr. T. That damn dog this, that damn dog that. You love that damn dog more than your own wife, is that it?

And my pops always with the same response, one hand resting on Mr. T's head, the other on the remote control: You know damn well that ain't true, Gerry. Hell, if this old dog here pissed and moaned at me half as much as you do, rest assured I'd've put him down long ago.

Mr. T was supposed to've been my dog before he became Daddy's dog. The old man'd adopted him out of the kill shelter for my eighth birthday. I was the one who'd named him Mr. T on account of Rocky III. He'd been half pit bull, half Rottweiler, this big old black and brown head, these pointy little ears cut straight up in the air. Daddy'd told me his fighting name'd been Killer Kowalski. He said Killer'd been the best damn fighting dog he'd ever bet on before the cops came in and ruined all the perfectly good fun.

To which Mama'd said, Jesus Christ, Larry. The boy's eight years old.

To which Daddy'd said, Ah for fuck's sake, Gerry. I try to do one nice thing for the kid... Daddy'd gone on to explain that Mama needed to stop babying me all the time or I'd never grow a pair. The boy needs a little responsibility. He needs to toughen up. And besides, Daddy'd said, patting the dog's head, the kid can learn a thing or two from a dog like this. Like how stand up for himself, and how not to get his ass bit.

Please, Mama, I begged and begged. Please, can I keep him, Mama? He'll be a good dog. I'll teach him.

To which Mama'd said no and no and no and uh-uh, no way. He'll rip your head off, baby. Which'd made me start crying. But then Mama'd come over and hugged me, half-whispered in my ear, Don't cry now, baby. Your daddy's gonna bring Killer here back to the shelter and bring you home something more appropriate. Like maybe a furry little kittycat. How's that sound?

To which Daddy'd said, are you trying to turn this kid into a homo? Is that your goal? And then they'd gone back and forth for a while before Daddy'd told Mama that they'd kill the dog if he brought it back, and Mama'd said,

Good, some dogs need to be put down, and then Daddy'd backhanded her one across the face and said, This is my house, goddamn it, and he is my son and I ain't gonna have him grow up sucking at his mama's tit 'til he's forty.

<hr>

***

What kind of man…? Mama starts to ask Uncle Lee, then trails off like she really wants to cry but she's out of tears. She tries once again to wrap her arms around him but he holds her at bay.

He asks again, How long, Geraldine?

I don't know, she says. That's what I'm trying to tell you, Lee. Everything went so fucking sideways. Robbie? he says turning back toward me at the table.

I've settled on staring at Mr. T by this time, trying to remember happy memories when he wasn't trying to snap my head off, my arms, my legs, even one time my little buddy fresh out the bathtub. I'm trying my best not to stare at the dark puddle around his paws and chest, trying my best not to look up past Daddy's pasty feet, the big gooey holes spilling out of the important life-giving places.

Yes sir? I say.

How long? Uncle Lee says.

A little after eight, I say. I remember cause I was in the basement watching TV and wrestling'd just come on, and I had the volume turned all the way up on account of Mama and Daddy fighting again, and then they'd stopped for a while and I'd thought it was done, but then I'd heard the shots, only I didn't come right away cause I'd figured Daddy was just drunk again and taking target practice of the back porch, and because it's the last show before Wrestlemania and I didn't to miss the Rock telling John Cena how he's gonna shove it up his candy ass.

Uncle Leland squints at me long and hard. Then he squints back at Mama then back at me. See? Mama says, pointing an accusing finger in my direction. See what I'm working with here?

***

Why can't just call the cops, Mama? I'm up to my feet now and I almost jump at the loudness of my own voice, pitch it hits when it cracks halfway through. From the looks Mama and Uncle Lee's faces, you'd a thought I'd just picked up Daddy's shotgun fired another round in him just for fun.

And tell them what, genius? Uncle Leland says after sharing a look with Mama for a beat or two.

The truth, I say. Like Mama says, Daddy was sick and abusive and had nothing to live for but she caught him trying to kill himself and tried to stop him. Risked her own life, trying to be the hero, but Daddy wouldn't let go of the gun and then Mr. T went and tried to chew her leg off and how that all ended up in one big tragic accident.

I step toward where Mama where she's now standing behind Uncle Lee, almost like she's afraid of me. It's the truth, ain't it, Mama? It about breaks my damn heart to see her suddenly so self-conscious around me.

It's like they say, Mama. We got the truth and truth'll set you free. Ain't that what you taught me?

I'll tell the cops, Mama. Tell them everything, everything you put up with from Daddy, everything you sacrificed to protect me. And even after all that, I'll tell them you were trying to save Daddy from himself. And it'll be the truth cross my heart and hope to die, and they'll see that and have to believe me, Mama.

Uncle Lee, he's standing between me and Mama like's he's her bodyguard. Back to me, he looks over his shoulder then back at her. Tells me, I can't count about fifty reasons for the cops'll think you're lying. He starts to count them off on his fingers one by one.

He's already to his ring finger before Mama steps out from behind him. That's enough, she says. Before that she reaches up and cups her hand to the side of his face, says his full name. Leland Joseph Barnes, she says, like she's scolding him but also soothing him. She says it low and slow, just over a whisper, the way she says my full name — Lawrence Robert Barnes Junior — whenever I get too fidgety and can't focus.

It strikes me as almost funny, the way she says it and the way Uncle Lee reacts. I swear I can see it in the way Uncle Lee's face goes soft in her hand as she whispers something to him I can't quite make out. *But Mama...*, I imagine him whining as she tells him what he can do to make whatever it is up to her. Probably she's telling him to apologize for yelling at me, telling him yelling never helps anything, telling him none of this is my fault, we're all hurting right now, we're all in shock, and searching for answers, trying to figure out what to do next.

Whatever she tells him, he shuts up and listens to someone else for the first time all night, and when she's done she gives him a little peck on the cheek same as she always does me when she tells me she loves me and she knows I have a good heart, I just got too much of my daddy in me sometimes.

***

Uncle Leland makes Mama practice her 911 call with him over and over before he'll let me give her the phone. He says things like You gotta get the gravel out your voice, Gerry. Show some frickin' range of emotion. And you can't just say oh no, oh no, oh no and hope the operator guesses what the hell you're blabbering about. You gotta stop screaming for somebody to help you and give them specifics. You know they're gonna record this, right? Play it over and over at the trial.

Mama eventually snatches the phone out of my hand and tells Uncle Lee she couldn't order a pizza right with this constant criticism. She tells him he shouldn't be here when she calls anyway. You've done quite enough already, she says, and you should be home when you get the call from the dispatch.

Besides, she says and shoots a wink in my direction, I got good old Robbie here for moral support.

Before Uncle Leland'll agree to head home—he only lives like two blocks down—he leans in and mutters something low and mumbly in her ear. Then she whispers something back in his ear. She touches him on the side of the cheek again and says just loudly enough for me to make out, But that doesn't make the little shit wrong.

***

She's pacing around the room and breathing heavy when she finally dials 911. Please, please, oh God please, he finally went and did it.

I can hear a woman scolding from the other end, Ma'am, ma'am, you need to calm down. Who did what? Please, ma'am I'm trying to help you but I can't if you won't calm down.

Just send someone, goddamn it, Mama shouts back into the phone. It's Larry… my husband. Christ, I think he's finally gone and done it. She stops to cough and then takes all these rapid-fire breaths from deep in her diaphragm like she might be about to hyperventilate or have a full-blown heart attack.

I need your address, ma'am, I can hear the woman still scolding on the other end. Take a deep breath and just tell me where you are.

I can't…, my mama says in between her breaths. I don't… Here, she says a second later, here's my son. Then handing the phone to me, she yells six inches from my face, *Robbie, it's 911! You need to tell them, you need to tell them where they need to send us help!*

***

It hasn't even been ten minutes of waiting for the cops, but Mama keeps telling me it'll all be okay. It'll be just like on teevee. She means *Dateline* or sometimes *48 Hours*. She doesn't care for all those fake cop shows like *CSI, NCIS,* or *Law & Order*, which were Daddy's favorites and which Uncle Leland would always razz him about.

You know none of this shit's real, don't you? he'd tell my Daddy. Hell, it's all serial killers, hot shit sexpots, and an unending supply of semen dripping from everywhere.

I've always been more of an action movie kind of guy, myself. If I'm not watching *Rocky* or *Rambo*, it's gonna be something like the first three *Die Hards*, *Beverly Hills Cop*, or *Lethal Weapon I* and *II*. As many times as Mama's come down to the basement to watch *Dateline* on my TV because Daddy wouldn't let her watch it upstairs, I never could figure what she saw in it. Everything's always so he said/she said and circumstantial evidence. Even after all these boring-ass trials and appeals and prison interviews, you never truly know if the guy actually killed his wife. Nobody ever takes the stand and confesses, and even when they do confess, it ends up getting thrown out because the guy hires some highly-paid *liars*, as Mama calls them, to argue that he only confessed because the cops interrogated him for twelve hours and promised him he could go home if only he'd admit he'd cut up his wife body into little parts, filled up several garbage bags, tied to cement blocks, and tossed them off a bridge somewhere late at night.

This is about sum-all of what I've learned from all the true crime shows I've sat through with Mama: Guys'll lie, cheat, steal, and beat on their kids and their old ladies, but when it comes down to it, they'd rather go to jail for the rest of their lives than pay for a divorce.

Mama says we'll both be fine as long as we stick to the truth, but then she also says that the truth doesn't mean we're gonna be stupid. It's like on TV, she says.

We're out back on the patio, Mama's pacing and smoking and rattling on and on. Uncle Leland's back with two other EMTs, and they've escorted us out of our own house and away from the blood and guts we've been staring at all night. Mama takes a drag, exhales out her nose, tells me the cops'll be here any minute.

I nod.

Do you trust me, baby?

I nod twice. I say, Yes, ma'am. I say.

Okay, Robbie, she says, but you know there's a big difference between telling the truth and telling them everything, right?

You understand that, baby?

I don't but I nod my head anyway. Whatever you say, Mama, I say.

No, Robbie, you don't get it, baby. They're gonna ask you over and over who shot your daddy and how a man trying to kill himself ends up with a whole in his head and his heart. They're gonna show you pictures of your daddy lying there dead, dead, dead, and a bloody mess. They're gonna say look at it, boy, look what you've done. They're gonna ask you why you waited three hours to dial 911. Where'd your mama get that black eye and broken ribs?

They're gonna ask you about that damn dog and what kind of boy can shoot not only his daddy, but his own dog.

They're gonna ask you if your daddy molested you and then they're gonna call you a dirty little pervert and a coward and say you been nothing but a pathetic little mama's boy your whole life and you blame your daddy for every bad thing that's ever happened to you and that's why you done snapped finally and took things into your own hands.

They're going get ugly with you, she says. They're going to try to twist the truth around until you start to question if you ever knew the truth in the first place, she says.

You understand what I'm telling you, baby?

I have to think on that for a moment. What's the truth and what's too much? I'd never had to consider this before. And who knew what truth and why then knew it, when they knew it, and whose fault that was. It was all very confusing now and I'd thought I'd seen it all on all those cop shows Mama made me watch.

I don't know, Mama, I say, because that's the truth.

And that's what you tell them, baby, she says. Puts her hand on my neck. You tell them over and over you don't know nothin' about nothin'.

But what about you, Mama? What'll be you telling them? What I want to ask, what I should've asked, but I don't get the opportunity because here comes Uncle Lee again only this time he's here on official business, the official business of pretending to try to save his brother, my daddy. This time with a somber, less angry look. He shakes his head, puts his hand on my shoulder like I'm suddenly a little kid again. He's real real sorry, he says. There was nothing they could do. It was too late.

Yeah, I think to myself, too little too late, Uncle Lee.

Mama, she lets out an *Oh God, Jesus* loud enough for the EMTs inside the house and any neighbors snooping around. Then: *No, no, oh God, no.*

If I didn't know Mama myself, I might even think the truth was she'd felt bad over what she'd done to Daddy.

I shake off Uncle Lee's hand and rush over to her side. I say again and again, it's okay, it's all going to be okay? She's not listening, too busy making looks as Uncle Lee, but I tell her anyway. Don't you worry, Mama. Daddy's in a better place now.

Mama goes on ignoring me. Shouts as shrill as she can muster: Can I see him? I need to see him. I need to tell him I'm sorry. I'm so sorry, Larry, she shouts into the house. Please oh please forgive me, honey, I was trying to save you.

Uncle Leland doesn't shout but says it loud enough to be heard: Geraldine, you don't need to go back in there. That's not Larry no more, that's not your husband.

Then to me: Robbie, whatever she tells you, you keep your mama outta here, okay? You're the man of the house now. It's time for you to do right by your mama for a change.

I nod a little but don't say yes sir. I don't salute him if that's what he's looking for. Honestly, I'm starting to like

Uncle Leland less and less as each new thing becomes known.

Then I get distracted. The sirens getting closer. I think we're all listening, all waiting. Uncle Leland puts his arm around Mama's shoulder, around my arm that's already around Mama's shoulders so that we're sandwiching her from both sides. He says he knows we're hurting and he's hurting too, but he has to go back inside and do his job. Larry would've wanted it that way, he says.

Before he heads back in, he leans in one more time in Mama's direction, one last squeeze of her shoulders, my arm around her shoulders, then a soft quick kiss to the top of her head.

It's all a bit too gushy for me, but then I scold myself for getting too cold and hard in the heart. Who am I to judge how people oughta grieve? I scold myself. Maybe Uncle Lee and Mama aren't blood family, but they're still family who've both just lost somebody, one a brother and the other a husband, and here I am judging them like one of them detectives from Mama's true crime shows, saying they ain't crying the way you're supposed to cry and all that.

I can hear a couple cop cars pull up at the front of the house, sirens blaring, doors slamming. I can hear them calling things in on walkie-talkies, but I can't hear what they're saying. Another minute goes by and I hear Uncle Leland shout loud and clear: We got a deceased white male, fifty-six years old, one gunshot to the head, another to the chest. Unresponsive upon arrival.

I can feel Mama leaning in and whispering in my ear, *You know what you need to do…*

And I'm not sure if she's asking or telling, but I nod but say nothing. Let my arm drop from her shoulder. I try to sneak a peek through the sliding glass doors to see if I can still see Daddy and what-all they're doing to him, what all's left of him.

Just you remember…, she whispers, but then she doesn't say nothing about TV or telling the truth. Your daddy was a sick sick man, she says, and your mama who loves you dearly risked her own life trying to save that worthless son of a bitch. And no matter what they might accuse me of, what they might say me or Lee or anybody might have accused you of, you don't believe a word they say for one instant. They'll try to turn you against your own mama, just to get you to change your tune.

You understand me? she asks.

I don't but I not anyway. My own little white lie.

And what are you going to tell them then?

I tell her because it's true. I say, Mama I'd never say anything to hurt you.

And she says, I know that, baby. I know that. But she never says it back or what she's gonna say when they lie and try to turn her against me. Which'll stick in my craw a little in the weeks, months, years to come.

Your no-good mama'd say anything save her own ass, they'll keep telling me. All these different cops, lawyers, my cellmates, all my new friends and family.

Stick to the truth and the truth will set you free, they'll say it same as Mama said it. Yeah, sure, but whose? That's the biggie, the thing that still gets me. And which one anybody'll believe when its two truths against one.

So Much Love

Here's the part where I tell you what a lousy bastard he was. I've seen the TV shows. I've got my lines memorized. Sure, but I'm trying to tell you that doesn't make me an actor either. Or my mother, my kid brother. How much of a sick son of a bitch our old man was. How he'd start out the night drunk and beating our ma, telling her how fat and useless she was, and end the night telling my little brother what a special, special boy he was.

Nine years old.

No clue what's right or wrong or what's gonna mess you up for forever.

No idea that your older brother knows better — as in, firsthand knowledge (is carnal the right word?) And still he does nothing to protect you. Says nothing. Repress, repress, repress. Buries that shit down deep and lets it fester while he tries to convince himself that it's not as bad at nine years old. Now knowing shit from a healthy childhood. Not as bad as it could get at thirteen.

The cliches, they keep coming. I'm telling you. I can't stop telling you. An embarrassment of cliches, my family, my life.

Like my mother, how she had no other options. What she had to tell herself. That he loved her but didn't know how to show it. That he loved us all so much he couldn't contain himself? That she could take all his love for the three of us and her two boys would never know> Would never hear the things coming out of their bedroom. The words, the sounds, the whole house quaking under the weight of his love, her love. Love love love destroying everything in its wake.

The lies she must've convinced herself to believe. That it was only her, that she was taking all his love so he'd have nothing left to give.

***

Listen. I'm telling you. I'm explaining.

He'd gone and messed with my little brother again. His thirteenth birthday. A rite of passage, he'd told him. Making a man of him, he'd told him. And that's how it'd gone from good touch/bad touch, to the whole nasty business. As in my little brother suddenly in my room crying and asking me point blank—no matter how hard I tried to avoid the question—Does that make me gay?

What I'm telling you, now, there was no more ignoring the questions, no more pretending I didn't know what I'd let happen, what our mother had let happen.

What I'm trying to tell you is I loved my brother, loved my mother. Obviously before all this I'd never considered how much or at what lengths I might go to prove it.

***

He was such a nice boy, somebody's saying on the TV somewhere. Maybe a little troubled, sure, but—but—

Nobody saw it coming is what they're all trying to convince you—you and me and themselves.

He must've snapped, they're telling you. They're on that big flat screen and they're telling you and anybody who'll listen: It wasn't our fault, it wasn't anybody's fault. Nobody could've seen it coming, they're telling you again.

It being how much I loved my mother and brother, what all I did to prove it to them.

All these TV shows and the cliches until who even knows what's true and what's just some sick sick crime show procedural where all they do is scream, rape, rape, rape until it finally comes true over and over and the same episode starts again.

***

Was it simply too much love? That's what I'd be asking if I were you. But I'm not, and it's no longer my story to tell. Events have transpired, events have taken my story and given it to you to decide.

His own parents, his little brother—what could've possibly happened behind closed doors?

Does anybody really believe in this whole troubled-teenager bit anymore, one more kid crying rape out into the five-hundred-channel/TV-on-demand, fifty-five inches of HD flat screen void?

Listen, what I'm trying to tell you: I wouldn't believe it either. It's simply too good to be true. No, wait. That's not entirely true either.

Notes on Jumping

Later on in the documentary, the interviewer asks the kid if he thinks it was a miracle.

According to her research, there've only been twenty-six other survivors. Which is pretty good really, she says, considering you hit the water going somewhere around seventy-five miles an hour, a force of a thousand pounds per square inch.

But I guess I don't have to tell you, she says. She even lets out a wry smile as she says it.

No, he'll say. She doesn't need to remind him.

She asks him what it's like falling over two hundred feet? She asks how many times he thought he'd died before he'd realized he'd survived?

He'll tell her about how long it took for him to resurface, how it'd felt. Like his lungs were exploding in slow motion. How one of his lungs actually had—or at least it had been punctured by one of his four broken ribs at least, so it was that along with his lacerated spleen.

How he'd just kept on kicking his feet despite the broken ankle he had, how despite his dislocated fingers on his right hand and shattered elbow on his left, he kept trying to flap his arms as hard as he could just the way his dad had once taught him to swim underwater.

He describes how painful that first gasp of air was once his head finally hit that surface, and then the sting of all that saltwater rushing in when his head bobbed under again. How he'll never be able to taste the salt of the ocean again without remembering the stabbing pain that shot through his chest as he let out that silent scream from deep down in his sour gut: *Ahh!* But no sounds would come out.

He pauses before describing the next part. He looks down for a moment and then back up into the camera. He says the next part is the part she probably won't believe, how nobody really believes it no matter how many times he tries to explain it.

You survived a jump from the Golden Gate Bridge, the interviewer says. She almost shouts it at him. Won't people believe just about anything after that?

The kid just shrugs.

Then he tells her about the school of dolphins. How they'd kept swimming back and forth under his feet to keep him afloat for twenty minutes until the Coast Guard could get there to pull him out.

And how he knows that God sent those dolphins. He pauses before nodding his head, to say yes, of course, he knows it was a miracle. How he knew God had sent him those dolphins so that he might live to spread the word of his experience and save others.

It's not like I don't realize how loony I sound, he tells the camera. How crazy it still sounds. I'd never even been to church a day in my life.

How weeks later, his mom and dad would sit him down and say they thought it was a bad idea for him to tell others about jumping and the dolphins sent from God.

You don't really want everybody out there to know what you tried to do to yourself, do ya, buddy? his dad had said.

Now honey, his mom had said, we just think it will be hard for people to understand when you tell them about the dolphins and how you think they were sent from God.

The kid makes sure to emphasize that his parents were both very thankful he'd survived and thought it was nice that he wanted to people, and of course they thought it was nice that he felt like he had a calling from a higher power.

The kid explains all this to the interviewer, then looks down at his hands folded in his lap. He sniffles a bit for the first time and shakes his head.

That's what's still so hard, you know? His voice cracks. To know how much I hurt my parents, right? And to know how much it embarrasses them. How much it hurts them that I would want to keep talking about it with others. How much they still don't trust me not to try to hurt myself again.

And that's what haunts him the most, he says. Just knowing how quickly after his fingers lost their grip on the railing, how quickly he knew that everything could've been fixed. How in the five long seconds he had to fall, the five seconds he'd had to think about what he'd done, it only took an instant for him to realize he didn't want to die anymore. Dear God, he'd kept saying to himself, I can't die! Dear God, I need to live!

She asks if the kid ever thinks about how many other jumpers, how many shooters, how many wrist cutters, how many of them may have had those exact same second thoughts that he'd had, and for how many of them it's too late, if he ever thinks about all the ones who *can't* fix it, *can't* undo what they've already done.

The kid looks up, then into the camera. He smiles. Why else would I be talking to you?

But what would you tell these people? She's grown a bit impatient. She can feel the moment she's been working for this whole interview, and she won't let it drop.

But what would you say to all these people? She asks. What would you say to the ones who haven't done it yet, but still might?

He doesn't say anything. Doesn't look up for the longest time. And when he finally does look up, to her, to the camera over her shoulder, the freckles under his eyes almost glisten under the lighting, his smile big and toothy, and then all lips.

He shakes his head ever so slightly. He looks back down into his hands folded in his lap, nods slowly to himself as if he'd just remembered the punchline to a joke he only now understood. A joke too crude to be shared in pleasant company.

Swiss

My Cousin Swiss says all he had to do was suck a little D and let them ink him up and the guys upstate basically left him alone.

This is why he has a Rubik's-Cube-sized swastika tattooed over his heart and why he can't stand gays. He doesn't say *gays*.

He's five years younger than me and a little over six months out on parole and I want to give him the benefit of the doubt that despite his casual homophobia and despite his four-inch-long blond chin beard, he isn't really a practicing member of the Aryan Brotherhood.

Or rather my ma really wants me to give him the benefit of the doubt and with Grandma's funeral tomorrow, I'm trying my best.

As if he's read my mind, Swiss pulls back his wife beater to reveal his swastika. Your ma says she's gonna help pay for me to get it covered up once everything with G'ma gets figured out. Get me a Biggie mean-mugging for the peeps. Underneath that the words Ready to Die.

He frames the words as if he's directing the movie of his life story.

In the voice of my mother, he says: We can't have you off looking for a job with that monstrosity, now can we?

He pounds his chest, kisses his fist, points two fingers up to the sky.

It's unclear if he's pointing up at Biggie or Grandma or both.

This swastika-tatted skinhead who used to be this gangly snotnosed four-eyed buck-toothed punk following me around every family get together to talk b-ball and hip hop and who had better flow Biggie or Tupac and who the third most important player on the Bulls was—Kukoc or Rodman.

Mostly I'd argue Kukoc just to piss him off.

For a cornfed midwestern white boy with a swastika prison tat, he's never much favored honkies.

I can only imagine the mental gymnastics he must've put himself through in prison.

We're out in the gravel driveway shooting hoops. Trying to stay out of all the family drama going on inside, the bickering about whose fault it was for not taking care of Grandma better and who hasn't paid their fair share of the funeral costs and who's gonna get the house or the money if they end up selling the house.

Swiss says it's what G'ma would've wanted. The two of us back hoopin' like the old days.

Probably her dying wish, I say.

I grab a beer from the garage and offer him one without thinking.

Ain't you heard, Cuz? he says. Old Swiss here's on the straight and narrow these days.

He's got a bottle of Mountain Dew—make that two bottles—one for drinking and one for dipping, because he's dipping while we're playing horse, and will continue to dip when we get to one-on-one and then to the inevitable scuffling.

It's a nasty habit, yo. But I'm trying to quit smoking and it's a bitch.

Shit I was a weed guy, he says, but then I got sent up and all there is to do is smoke and work out and do your time.

He's put on maybe twenty, thirty pounds of muscle from the last time I saw him. Grandpa's funeral fifteen years earlier, that last time before Uncle Frank's funeral five years earlier.

No longer the caved-in chest, no longer the bony shoulders and chicken wings for arms. Though in the year since he's been out, some of the muscle's already started to melt into fat and stretchmarks around his belly.

Still got those jacked up teeth from childhood, which with the meth have only gotten more jacked over time. Excluding the dental bridge my ma paid for to replace his two missing bottom teeth.

Over the last few years, ma having taken up the mantel of babying him after Grandma got put in the home. But she'd always had a soft spot for him, everything he's gone through, and her being a Registered Nurse and the only one in the family who falls above the poverty line.

Nurse Sharon out to save her white trash family one dollar at a time! What Swiss's old man likes to say. That and: Nurse Sharon swoops in to rescue us again!

Uncle Randy being the baby of the family, my ma being the eldest and my grandma's favorite, the only one who went to college and got out.

You keep babying that boy and he's gon' end up shittin' on you for the rest of his life.

With that boy being Swiss. And babying him being all the excuses Ma and Grandma made for him growing up.

But he's got such a good heart... Uncle Randy used to tease my ma and Grandma. But he's such a nice boy...

Just because it was coldhearted doesn't mean Randy didn't have a point.

One part of his point being that six years ago Swiss'd convinced the whole family into believing he had cancer when really he was strung out on meth and needed more money.

Another part being Swiss stealing checks from Grandma to feed his meth habit.

And Swiss selling meth out of Grandma's garage for nearly six months before he got caught.

Not caught for selling drugs. Caught for holding up his own dad's NAPA store and sticking a very real-looking squirtgun in his stepmom's face from behind the counter. Tammy literally pissing her pants, Swiss and his two other tweaker buddies pulling up on snowmobiles right before close and wearing ski masks and speaking in what Swiss calls his Shaq-voice demanding Tammy to empty the till for them.

This the only thing Swiss says he doesn't regret— scaring the shit out of Tammy that gold-digging bitch.

All that still the refrain of yeah but's:
Yeah but he doesn't know any better...
Yeah, but it was the drugs that made him do it...
Yeah, but it's a disease, you know...

Meaning the meth addiction, of course, not the faked cancer.

But with Swiss it could mean so many other things too: the disease.

***

Get a load of this one, he says. Tosses the ball up and then headbutts it in off the backboard like a trained seal. He ends up knocking his glasses off in the process, but still the goofy skill is there.

I shake my head and tell him to fuck off with that circus shit. I don't even try the shot for fear of making myself look like Swiss or making myself look like I'm lowering myself to Swiss's level even as I can't meet him at his level.

I'll take the H, I say.

Nobody's watching so far as I can see, but then it's not just about seeing people see me. It's about me seeing myself at my age making an ass out of myself. It's about the motion sensor on the flood light flicking on and off randomly as you try to navigate your way to the rim. It's about the potentiality of me messing it up and breaking my nose or worse.

Guys upstate used to hate playing horse with me, he says, cleaning the dust off his glasses. Run it on them and collect my cigs without so much as a ho.

Upstate, what Swiss calls prison, the way he'll do anything to not call it prison. Not so much out of an embarrassment level, I don't think. More so a hip-hop credo to not call anything by its actual name.

His second shot he cradles the ball behind him on his lower back and somehow lofts it up over his head and banks it in.

Which makes me a ho, which Swiss is not above reminding me. You's a ho, Cuz. You's a low-down dirty ho, he says. Then he winks and says, Just fuckin' wit ya'.

The light flickering off his glasses make his eyes look like mini-TVs as smudgy windows into his soul.

**

Before his next shot, Swiss calls time out to rummage around Grandma's garage for something. A minute later he appears again with a pockmarked-tooted smirk and my old boombox.

Chickety-check it, yo, he says.

It's not just the boombox. He's got my old Tupac CD. Greatest Hits. Pac's greatest hits being what whiteboy wannabes like me got when we were trying out our black cred and didn't have any other black kids around to call us on our Yo MTV raps bullshit.

Thought G'ma threw it out, didn't ya? But thank old Swiss'y here to save the day, done snatched it out of the trash when she wasn't looking.

Turn that trash off this instant, he says in his Grandma voice.

We Swensons might be a lot of things, I say in my own Grandma voice, but we are not some gangster trash.

Old G'ma always hatin' on the rap game, Swiss says.

Old Grandma with her casual white trash racism. I don't say that but I think it. I think about the mental gymnastics Grandma must've had to do to ignore Swiss's love of all things black.

Not that Grandma was on board for the Aryan stuff either. Ish ish ish, she'd say about Siss's swastika. Have you seen what those Nazi's have done to my poor Scottie?

Swiss plays Amerika's Most Wanted and then starts in on these buddies of his he had upstate. You should'a heard them, Cuz. Dem Krazy White Boyz. Dudes spittin' rhymes like hardcore black guys from the hood.

He doesn't say black guys.

This is new for Swiss. This n-word this and n-word that. And the f-word for gays. At least it's new to me. And I'm not entirely sure how to handle it—to call him out or just let it slide.

I can't decide if it's something Grandma'd say ish ish ish about or if it'd be the type of thing she'd look past in favor of keeping the peace.

I used to be an assistant principal. We didn't have any black kids in the school, but we still had guest speakers and racial tolerance videos.

I decide Grandma would want me to let it slide for her sake.

***

Swiss tells me I'd've done all right up there.

He means in prison.

He means it as a compliment. The fact that I still shave my head even if these days it's more of sad necessity of my receding hairline.

The fact that I've shed the beer gut and muffin top since I lost my job and started working at the Y, since my wife left me and took the kids, since I moved back home to take care of ma's house while she moved back to her home to take care of Grandma.

You know, I think you'd've done alright up there, Cuz. He's looking me up and down while combing through his chinbeard. I'm raining jumpshots from back by the bushes and sporting my old coaching polo and matching team wind pants, not exactly gang colors.

It doesn't not make me feel a little better about myself and the gutter I've climbed into these past years.

Dude, he says and nods back over his shoulder, the fam' is straight trippin' up in the hizzou.

My ma's family's typical loud talking and hooting and hollering going on inside. All four remaining siblings, my ma and three uncles, their wives and girlfriends and kids and stepkids, the Cubs game on full blast.

It takes a certain level of white trash bluster to get midwestern folks rowdy enough to let the neighbors hear your business. My ma's family is that level of white trash.

***

Two years ago, while Swiss was sucking a lil' d and getting a swastika tattoo, I was the head girls basketball coach and assistant principle at a big city high school four states away from here.

I was married to my high school sweetheart and had two sweetheart daughters, four and six years old.

I was living the life, and far, far away from all this trash family drama.

Then one of my players accuses me of spying on girls showering and giving more playing time to the more well-endowed.

It isn't true, at least never intentionally and never more than an accidental glance out of the corner of my eye having to bring in more towels or grab the jerseys to wash.

After the initial outcry, the rest of the girls back me up and eventually the girl confesses that she was just pissed off over playing time, but then there's really no putting that genie back in the bottle.

It only takes two weeks of indefinite suspension and rumors spreading like wildfire before Kath is telling me she can't in good conscience raise two young girls under my household—even if she could believe me.

She doesn't wait around for the exoneration story they run on the back sports page.

It's not like they put it on the front page when the headline is: Turns out it was just another angsty teenaged girl who lashed out at a male authority figure.

A Good Ram Is Hard to Find

I haven't seen my girls in months and I haven't been on a date since and my ex-wife won't return my late night drunk dials and here I am inching ever closer toward 40 and still wearing my coaching outfit and playing horse with my meth-head cousin the night before my grandma's funeral.

***

You get older, you get your own life, move away, that's what family becomes. Waiting for people to die to see them again.

I try to explain this to Swiss when he asks why I never came around to see Grandma before she died.

He says, Nah, man, that your shit. That ain't family. Fam is blood, fam is forever. When he says forever he throws up some kind of cross-fingered gang sign, but not an Aryan gang sign—if the Aryan Brotherhood even has gang signs.

Swiss says the two of us, we're like brothas from anotha mutha.

It's not my favorite of all the colorful expressions that come out Swiss's mouth, but it's not completely wrong either.

Twenty years ago my old man had an affair with Swiss's mom and then kept having the affair with her after they got caught. A year later the two of them run off to start a new family in Florida twenty hours away. The two of them and however many of kids they got now wanting nothing to do with me or Swiss.

This is my family.

I've spent most of my adult life trying to forget about all of them—even at times, my own ma.

And I'd been doing a pretty good job of it too until the showering accusations and me having to tuck my tail and run back home to take care of my ma's place while she took care of grandma.

Swiss says he don't trip about all that old drama. Life's too short, yo, he says. Gotta brush it off your shoulders, he says and brushes off his shoulders while beatboxing to Jay-Z lyrics.

Just look at fuckin' Randy, he says. G'ma's dead and all that dipshit can think about is his big sis making him look bad again. And for what? For taking care of G'ma the last month? For paying all her bills and planning her funeral?

Which's fucked up, yo, he tells me, because your moms' is a good-ass woman. You know she was the only one to visit me upstate?

Swiss says all this shit with Randy saying that she'd been trying to turn G'ma against the rest of the family ain't nothin' but your ma takin' one for the team. No matter what bullshit Randy is on. He never could let nothin' go.

Sheet... Randy still ain't never forgiven me for holding up his store and that was five years ago. I did my time. What I'm thinking is if the state's satisfied, then I'm thinking my own daddy could find it in his heart. Hell, he was the one who taught me how to cook.

Cook meth, he means. He means how Randy'd tried his own hand at making a buck back in the day when he was still getting paid under the table as a grease monkey at my Uncle Clay's garage a couple towns over.

And that bitch Tammy, he says. Don't get me started.

Tammy being his mother-in-law who's two years younger than him and used to be his tweaker booty call. Tammy being the one he'd threatened to pop a cap on in the process of robbing his dad's business.

Here's Swiss not getting started on Tammy: One day I'm getting Randy to give her a job, the next day she's giving me handies under the table in the breakroom in exchange for oxys. The next day after that she's showing up with a big old baby bump and telling everybody it's Randy's.

Speaking of whores, he says getting back to our game.

He drops the ball out on the street past the driveway, lets it bounce, and then tries to punt it in from long range. It's straight on but sails five feet over the backboard bouncing up over the top of the garage.

Damn wind, he says. Bitch was dead on.

I say, Regular goddamn hurricane we got here.

I've ridden out Swiss's initial barrage of circus shots, holding steady as a HO, Swiss a less-than-focused HOR. Swiss who can bounce it between his legs backwards and bank it in from three but can't make a fifteen-foot jumpshot to save his life. Can't do anything that's not half-baked, or in his case, full-on baked.

Incoming, he hollers from the other side of the house.

Nearly sinks it too, sailing maybe a foot too long over the back of the backboard but dead on.

Story of Swiss's life. When it's not his turn, he's a foot too long. When it is his turn, he's over the roof.

***

Swiss so named Swiss because back when he was a kid and had a stutter and couldn't pronounce his name—Sco-Sco-Sco-tee-tee-tee... Sweh-Sweh-Sweh... Swenson.

How do you not feel the littlest bit of pity for a sad-sack story like that? It ain't easy for a kid named Swiss—the country song they should've written about the Swiss's fucked up family—with Swiss's family being my family.

Swiss whose mother abandoned him before he turned five to run off with his uncle—my father. Swiss whose teenaged father would pawn him off on our seventy-year-old Grandma so he could go out and chase tail, cook meth, and look for his next teenaged bride.

***

Swiss whose own family took to calling him Swiss, same as the little shits who mocked his stutter so unmercifully back in elementary school.

Swiss who still can't stand swiss cheese to this day and did so before he ever got the name—refused to eat anything but Kraft American yellow, no matter what Grandma would do to get him to broaden his tastes.

Broaden his tastes with swiss cheese.

Mash potatoes instead of French fries.

Milk instead of Mountain Dew.

Swiss only doubling down whenever she'd put her foot down and say he wasn't allowed to drink any more pop unless he'd drink his milk first.

He'd take the glass of milk in one hand and a bottle of Dew in the other and pour them down his throat simultaneously without so much as gagging.

How stubborn Swiss has always been to do things his own ass-backward way.

***

Back in the summer after I graduated from high school, my ma paid to have Swiss come up to basketball camp with me. I was coaching the middle schoolers for a few extra bucks before college in the fall, and my ma thought it'd be nice to pay for Swiss to come up and go to camp, get him away from some of the bad influences he was hanging out with. And maybe I could teach him a thing or two.

He shows up with pink hair, the words Bad Boy scribbled in black dye on the side of his head like a second-grader learning cursive for the first time.

This is Swiss, I have to tell the rest of the coaches and players. This is my cousin.

It's not even that Swiss didn't have talent. He had six-two talent in eighth grade. Had this hairy-legged

European game to him. The big man with the pop-bottle glasses and pink hair who could dribble it behind his back, snap a no look pass, do the finger roll, the tear drop, the leaping leaner. Somehow both gawky and smooth at the same time.

If he hadn't been such a goddamn goof. If he hadn't been so goddamn averse to the basics, the fundamentals. In other words, everything you go to camp to learn, everything my old man had drilled me on before he ran off with Swiss's ma.

The basics, fundamentals. Do the right thing and sooner or later you'll get the right results, my old man would say. There's no way to showboat your way to the top.

You'd think that in light of the old man abandoning me, I would've rejected his old school doctrines, but in reality it only made me more zealous about them.

Me being nothing special, especially when it came to height or athleticism. Not the tallest, not the smallest. Not the slowest, not the quickest. All heart.

Another word for it being okay, mediocre, unmemorable.

I'd convinced myself that was why my old man had had such an easy time running out on me.

If I'd had Swiss's height, I'd tell myself If I'd had Swiss's ability to block out everything and play real basketball like it was NBA Jam basketball...

Imagine how far I could've gone if I'd been Swiss and applied my old man's teachings.

I'm telling myself this every day I take Swiss to camp with me. Tell him to make ten free throws—balance, eyes, elbow, hold the follow-through. Watch him clang eight out of ten without even bothering to dribble in between.

Tellin' you Cuz, he tells me—me being his coach. I ain't about these free throws, yo. I got too much Bad Boy in me. Got that Worm in my blood.

By Worm he means Dennis Rodman aka the OG badboy. Swiss's words.

Like everything with Swiss, there'd always be just enough to make you want to root for him despite all the reasons to want to see him fail and maybe finally learn from his failures.

One time down the court, you'd watch him flow from one end to the other spot a teammate under the hoop out of the back of his head, do a little shimmy, a little shake, an okey-doke inside-out dribble shell game with his opponent. Flip it between the defender's legs and hit the cutter right in stride for a layup.

Next time down the court you'd watch him put it between his legs and dribble it off his foot nobody within fifteen feet.

Look over at me on the sidelines and shrug. A little too much jam in my jelly on that one, he'd say.

Don't trip, yo, he'd say. Got homeboy set up for the next time. Ain't even gon' see me comin' next time. Say that while waving his hand in his face—you can't see me—while homeboy's going in for an unguarded lay up on the other end.

Next time, always the next time.

***

The nail in my coffin is Swiss dunking it off the garage.

Doesn't just dunk it either. He flips it up over his shoulder, kicks off garage door, catches it in the air, and tomahawks it.

Comes down and does this silverback gorilla thing, pounds his chest. Gets up in my face and hollers, Ahh...! and How do you like that, Cuz? Huh? Huh?

Then a second later: Ah, just fuckin' wit ya, bro.

Make you feel like a big man? I say. Six-four and still jumping off Grandma's garage?

You wanna see old Swiss-Diesel throw it down for real? Is that what I'm hearing from ya, Cuz?

I wanna see you just once cut the goofing around and try a shot you could make in a real game.

You wanna see old Swiss-Diesel punk you in primetime live? Is that it?

A moment later: Ah, just fuckin' wit ya. You don't gotta to match all that. Mess around and break your hip, old man.

I tell Swiss enough with this horse shit. Let's say we settle this like men.

Oh it's like that, eh?

Mono-e-mono.

A Good Ram Is Hard to Find

Cuz on Cuz?

Let's call it prison ball rules just to make it interesting.

Oh, you think you all hard core like that now?

He's smiling big and wide with them buckteeth, that straggly-ass chin beard, the glare of the floodlights reflecting off his pop bottle glasses.

He spits dip in one bottle and takes a swig of Dew with the other.

May the better man win, he says and tosses me the ball. With his snus in it sounds like he's Rocky with the mouthguard in.

Ladies first, I say, tossing the ball back.

Nah, he says, age before beauty.

Style versus substance, I say.

For the honor of the Swenson family name.

Yeah, I say. And loser has to tell Randy that baby ain't his.

***

Much to the irritation of both my ma and my pops, Randy was actually my favorite uncle growing up.

I might've done everything I could to try to dissuade Swiss from following me around, but at the same time, I'd be begging for Uncle Randy to come hang out downstairs, away from the bickering of the rest of the adults.

And usually he'd oblige. He'd leave his wife to deal with the grownup talk upstairs and sneak off down to the basement to grab a beer and his rolling papers from out the bedroom he still kept at Grandma's.

He'd come out and wrestle with us, use Swiss as a dummy to demonstrate the finishing maneuvers like the four-figure leg lock or the camel clutch.

Play NBA Jam and NBA Live. Smoke his weed and drink his beer and never lose his temper like my old man would.

Always telling us inside jokes about my ma marrying my father.

You know your ma never met a three-legged dog she didn't want to bring home and nurse back to health.

Your ma, she might be the smartest one in the family but she sure know how to pick him.

Your ma, she gone to school for eight years to be a nurse and still can't figure a way to surgically removed that stick out your dad's ass.

Randy with all his jokes, and don't get me wrong, they were funny—at least at the time—but also, I wonder if he ever thought back on those after my old man ran away with his first wife.

***

It's past nine o'clock when he saunters outside to smoke a bowl with Clay, Duey, and Melvin. When he sees us still hooping, he says, Shit, y'all bitches still out here hoopin'. Then he says, Well hell then, and hollers over for Swiss to hoop him. He points up towards the rim with a bottle of beer and takes a couple wobbly-kneed steps in his cowboy boots and gathers himself.

Swiss winking at me with that watch this kind of wink. Flips it with one hand up toward the rim and hits his old man right in the hands—or rather, hand—Uncle Randy holding onto a bottle of beer in one hand, he somehow manages to tap the ball with the other, only to have it clank the bottom of the rim and ricochet off his face, him losing his balance in the process and ass-planting the gravel in front of the garage.

Damn.... Randy, Swiss says.

Uncle Clay, Duey, and Melvin stop smoking long enough to say the same thing. Damn... Randy.

Their kids, their kids' kids and all the step-kids behind them they don't say anything, probably wondering whether to laugh or flee to the basement for fear of a scuffle.

Randy flat on his back under the hoop. To his credit or to his deficit, he's held onto the beer that's foaming all over him.

Jesus Christ, he's hollering and turtling around on the driveway. You liked to've killed me, wouldn't ya, boy?

What'd ya need me for? Swiss says. Looks like you done a pretty good job yourowndamnself.

Clay and the others laughing even harder now, smoking and laughing. Pregnant Tammy waddling her way through the onlooking kids and grandkids to come out for a look.

Damn it, Randy! Tammy hollers. She's got her soon-to-be youngest in the oven and current youngest on her hip, two more rugrats in tow, as she's shooting daggers in Swiss's direction. Happy now? those daggers are saying to Swiss in between her cursing Randy out for making her look like an ass again in front of his family. That and giving Swiss the satisfaction.

By then my ma's found her way out too.

Don't you think you're too old to be messin' around with the boys, Randy?

Randy, ignoring her, takes a swig of foamy beer, spits it out, and points it at Swiss. You think you're some hot shit, eh boy?

Swiss hollering, Yo you played yo'self, son! Then grabbing his junk or where his junk would be if his jean shorts weren't hanging halfway down his ass.

Starts rapping: You better chickity-check yo'self before you wreck yo'self.

Uncle Randy bottle still in hand and one arm on Tammy to stay upright. You don't even belong here, you little shit, he slurs. What all you did to Grandma, broke her goddamn heart, what she got for babying you all these years.

Stop it! my ma yelling louder than I've ever heard her yell. Can't you two get along? For one night? For Grandma?

Things go silent except for Tupac droning on from the boombox about having sex with Biggie's wife.

Everyone is staring at her now. Then staring back at Randy then back at her. It's like the teacher has just gotten back from the hallway to break up the classroom fight.

Mostly everyone waiting to see who the first one would be to talk shit back to the teacher.

It's Randy: Well, thank the lord almighty, here she comes again to save the day. Nurse Sharon swoops in to rescue us from—

What stops him from saying the next thing is the basketball smacking him right in the kisser. Another no-look pass from Swiss right on the money. Uncle Randy back down for the count.

***

Uncles Clay through Melvin eventually waking up a woozy Randy, picking him up, and escorting him off the court and out to his truck for Tammy drive him home.

If he remembers Swiss knocking him silly with the basketball, he's not saying anything and neither is anybody else. Everybody else—including Tammy—just happy to get Randy home before he makes things any uglier than they already are heading into the funeral the next morning.

Swiss watching the whole thing go down with that buck-toothed, pock-marked shit-eating grin on his face.

Hey yo, he whispers to me. Wanna know why I done robbed that dipshit?

Meth? I say.

Nah, he whispers. That's what everybody thinks but it wasn't actually the drugs. Or... not completely.

Shits and giggles? I say.

Nah, he says, but yo, it did make me feel sorta fuckin' good for once, feel me?

I ain't feelin' you.

Hurting them back finally, he says. I mean I wasn't about to blast the bitch between the eyes or nothing. But it wouldn't've broke my heart if I'd gotten a chance to pop a cap in that boney little ass of hers.

Lucky for her I only had the piddly-assed squirt gun on me, he says. Otherwise she'd be walking even funnier than she already does with that meth baby of hers.

Nah, I say. You wouldn't've done that. You ain't got the heart for it.

Probably not, he says. But it'd've been pretty funny, wouldn't've?

Not to Randy it wouldn't've.

Yeah, he says. And that's the whole point.

***

Long as I can remember my ma nagging on me about how important it was for me to be a positive male role model in Swiss's life. What with Randy being Randy.

My grandma the same thing.

Always with that cliché about giving back to those who don't have the advantages, this whole idea that if only Swiss'd been my actual brother instead of my cousin, how things might've turned out different.

Except it wasn't like I was feeling all that privileged back then growing up without a dad. Throw in the fact that he'd run off with Swiss's ma and I wasn't about to put my arm around him and lead him down the path of the straight and narrow.

And where had that path gotten me?

One long guilt track on repeat.

If you could only talk to him... If you could only hear how remorseful he is, how broken up he is about all the people he's hurt.

If you could only see him... See how depressed he is behind bars. How hard it must be for him to survive in there. Don't you remember how sensitive he was?

You know full well that he's not made for this. He's not tough like that. He's just a kid still, just that same sweethearted kid he always was.

Such a sad thing, the way that drugs can get into you and make you do things.

But I know Swiss'd really appreciate a letter from you...

Don't you remember ow much he's always looked up to you...?

Sure, I remember.

But also: I remember.

And anyway, what does one write to a cousin who's gone to prison for trying to rob his own dad and threatening to shoot his own stepma?

I don't know how I'd gotten to a place in my life where I'd be emailing a cousin in prison to console him. And I wonder if it was a bigger surprise to him or me.

I should've written sooner, I write. I've just had this stuff with my job and now Kath and the girls.

But I should've been there for you more when you needed help.

I tell him to keep his head up in there. Or maybe keep your head down? Not sure what's best to surviving in there.

Anyway, everybody out here is rooting for you, I lie.

I tell him we all know that you were just doing what you thought you had to to survive. It's a disease.

The lies you have to tell your family to keep up the charade.

I ask Swiss if he remembers that basketball camp when I coached him?

I never told you then, but I was so proud to be your cousin that week. To see how you could play the game the way nobody else played the game and you didn't get caught in all the little shit.

I end it by apologizing again for not writing sooner. From now on, I tell him, I'm going to be a better cousin.

I sign it –one life, one love, your cuz.

A week later I get an email from the prison saying a prisoner would like to email you and if it's okay to forward it on.

I never reply back.

***

Yo how come you ain't got them girls with you?

With their ma, I say.

A Good Ram Is Hard to Find

We're on another snus break. I have my back turned to him. I'm practicing my follow-through. Flipping the ball up in the air and watching the backspin under the lights as it comes back to me. I'm thinking about all the times I've done this in my life, how I used to lie in bed at night and listen to my parents fight and flip the basketball up over and over practicing the perfect form—the perfect swan neck, hold the follow-through.

Your moms done told me about what all went down with your job.

I don't say anything. I try my best to ignore him and hope he'll let it drop.

He doesn't.

Yo, that's shit's fucked... up.... And now your old lady won't even let you bring the girls for G'ma's funeral?

Yeah, I say finally. Kath got pretty freaked about all of it. Even after it all played out, I don't think she ever fully believed me. Hell, I don't think she ever trusted me in the first place. Coaching high school girls. Always staying after practice to get in one-on-one drills with them. I tried to tell her it was just to make them better. It's what my old man used to do to me. I'd do the same thing for our girls when they grew up.

She always said it wasn't natural. A man my age spending so much time around teenaged girls instead of his own daughters.

Swiss: And all because some jailbait bitch accused you of sneaking peeks?

Yo, I say, I'm not really trying to think about that all right now. It's too goddamn much to be thinking about and now with Grandma... You feel me?

Shit, yeah, I feel that, he says out of the side of his snus. He goes on to tell me about this old MILF he used to supply/hook up with before he went upstate.

Three-spoons-a-day keeps reality at bay, he says. Morning, lunch, and dinner and three shorties at home with two different baby daddies, none of them mines. And I'm not even sweatin' it, yo. I'm treatin' them youngins as if their mine. Treatin' them the way G'ma treated me. And all the while I'm trying to get her clean—me!—I'm the one trying to keep her on the straight and narrow. I'm refusing to take her money or feed her habit. And all for the sake of them shorties.

After a while bitch is leaving me home to babysit five nights a week so she can go bartend, shake her tits, and trade free drinks for drugs from my competition.

And what do I get for my troubles?

Bitch won't even let me come over to drop off Christmas presents.

If you don't mind, let's cut the sob story bullshit and just play ball, cool?

He's taking a swig of Dew and not looking when I throw the ball a little harder than I want to and catch him in the gut. I can see him swallow a little tobacco and start to gag.

Damn Cuz, he says coughing. You ain't gotta be like that. I'm just trying to say I feel ya.

You feelin' this? I say getting up in his grill.

He palms the ball and holds up above his head like he's going to pull some Harlem Globetrotters shit and I'm the old white guy ref jumping and waving his hands.

Be honest, though, he says with a wink. You sneaked a little peek, didn't ya? Tell me you didn't scope out a few pairs of them sweet little teenaged titties before they ran you out, you dirty old dog you.

I'd haul off and deck the skinhead motherfucker right here right now. Lord knows I've thought about it before. Thought about it from the time the kid was old enough to talk all his smack. Role model? Shit. Tough love. Knock some sense into him. Teach him to shut his mouth once in a while and focus on the task at hand.

And maybe if it was anything but Grandma's funeral, I would haul off on him. If it was anywhere but here with my ma inside and how I've been a lousy son my whole life and how she's the only one I got left in my life who doesn't think I'm a pedophile.

Don't worry, Cuz, he says and winks at me one more time. Secret's safe with me. You and me, we keep it family, yo.

I lunge for the ball over his head, maybe I'm lunging for his face in the process. I let myself go for his fake. Like that ref at the Globetrotters' game, I let him punk me. Watch him flip the ball over my head, take two dribbles, and go in for a dunk. A Doctor J rock the cradle off the garage.

Ah…! he hollers when he comes down. You reach I teach, boy. Ain't that what you used to tell me?

This is where I am in my life. I'm taking my own lessons back from my meth-head cousin.

So I resort to the only thing I have left to resort to. I play dirty. Jab my forearm into his lower back. Get me a good handful of his wife-beater, you can hear it ripping a little with every move he tries to make. And when goes up for one of his dunks, I shoulder-check his ass into the garage.

Not trying to injure him or nothing. Just enough to remind him that I might be a has-been, but I'm still the big dog in this relationship.

Which he clearly doesn't like.

Or isn't ready for.

Or doesn't expect me to stoop to.

Okay, okay, okay, he keeps saying. You want the d-o-double-g? you gon' get the d-o-double-geezy.

Except he doesn't really have it in him. Or he doesn't have it in him to get dirty with me.

Or he's still feeling pity for me. How pathetic it is, the old dog trying to keep the young pup down for one more day.

Either way I only get more chippy that he won't fight back.

A Good Ram Is Hard to Find

That I'm five years older than him and he's the one with the prison record and no job, no other home to go to, the night before the funeral of the grandma he stole from, the grandma he abandoned, the grandma he convinced he had cancer just to get more money and pity than she was already giving him.

Here I am and here he is and here we are together, and I'm the one having to play dirty to get over.

***

And yet here we still are nearing midnight. The floodlight from the garage one of the only lights still on in the neighborhood, our shadows fifteen-feet tall on the driveway.

Tupac's Greatest Hits having long ago played out, neither of us willing to be the one to restart it. It's silence for all I can hear save for my heart pounding in my ear, Swiss's labored breathing next to me. Everybody having gone home or out to the bars except for me, Swiss, my ma, and the ashes of our dead grandma.

Me and Swiss in best out of seven, game tied up nine-nine heading for eleven, win by two.

I'm running on nothing but piss and vinegar at this point. But I have the ball and I've decided I need this. I've lost the only job I ever wanted. My wife is gone, my little girls probably don't remember who I am. My grandma's dead.

And what's one more L in Swiss's book? Hell, he doesn't even care. He's never cared. That's the whole thing with Swiss. He's never taken anything serious enough to cut the shit and do things the right way.

And tonight's just one more example of it.

I hit him with the only thing I have left in my repertoire. My step-back fadeaway from long range a la Larry Bird. But even that I can't just stick it in his eye. I have to throw the junk at him. Jab step, ball fake, rocker step, and then shot fake part two.

In other words, I pull out the old man tricks. And because he's still the young buck with too much energy to bury me once and for all, he goes for it. Tries to swat my shit the way he's been swatting my shit all night.

What I've been setting him up for this the whole night. At least I'm telling myself this now that I've already set things in motion.

Problem is even after I give him everything I got, get him up in the air and flying by, he's so damn tall and lanky I can't get a shot off.

I could lean in and draw the foul. We could argue about that. He could give me shit about no cheap fouls in prison ball.

Or… I could lean into it being prison ball and take things into my own hands.

This is what I'm telling myself when I undercut Swiss on his way down—as I lean in and hit him with my shoulder to his ribs, as I knock him off his feet, as I watch him hit the deck face first into the gravel.

As I wink at him and line up the shot. Game, I say before I even let it go.

I'm still holding my follow-through when it goes through the net. Just like my old man used to tell me. Keep it up there, hold up that swan neck 'til you see it go through the rim.

I don't get in his face and holler like he would, but I'm not offering him a hand to help him up off the driveway either. I'm still holding that swan neck as if to make an example.

This, this is what you need to do if you're going to be a real ball player. You need to take things seriously. You need to focus on the little things, the basics.

We're back at basketball camp some fifteen years earlier and I'm trying to teach him a proper jump shot the way my father taught me the proper jumpshot. Only Swiss's not listening. He's thinking about… I don't know what he's thinking about. I've never known what he's thinking about.

But I'm the coach and he's the player and all I know is that he's not thinking what he's supposed to be thinking and I'm thinking why even try if he's not going to try.

Why take the time? Why try to give a damn? Why me? Why can't I have all the natural talent that's wasted on him?

I eventually let my follow-through drop as I watch Swiss dust off his wifebeater and jean shorts, pick up his glasses off the ground and himself.

Damn, Cuz, he says rubbing the scratches on his face. That's cold. That's some straight-up dagger-to-my-heart-type shit right there.

For a moment me and Swiss are both standing and catching our breath and staring at the rim where I've just put the nail in his coffin.

The ball's rolled off into the bushes and neither of us is planning on getting it. We're done. It's over.

Right on cue, the motion light sensor flicks off and leaves us in the dark.

Sorry, I say. I guess I got a little too caught up, you feel me?

Nah, man, he says. Ain't no apologies in prison ball. He comes over in the dark and drapes his lanky arm over my shoulders. That right there, he says poking me in the chest, that's the shit I'm talking about, Cuz. That's what I was always telling guys back upstate when they'd ask me who taught me to ball. I'd say, yo, my cuz a straight-up hardcore baller shot caller. He don't play, I'd say. He a cold-blooded killer.

He grabs my hand with his hand. He pulls me to him, dabs me up. I missed you Cuz, he says.

Swiss is many things but he's not my dad and this is not the emotional validation I'm looking for, but there I am tearing up anyway as I stand there and let him hold me in his lanky-ass, sweaty arms.

And there I am, when he starts to let go, refusing and pulling him back to me. Pulling his shoulders and chest down to my chest, wrapping my other arm around his back, pounding the small of his back with my fist—soaking wet polo shirt pressed up against wifebeater. I'm feeling our hearts beating against each other. I'm feeling my tears fall on his scratchy chin beard.

I just miss her, you know? I just miss her so much.

Yo, I feel you, Cuz, he says. I feel you.

At some point, my ma comes out and the light flicks back on. She tells us she's going to bed and not to stay out too late. We've got to get to the church by nine the next morning.

But before that she stands there in her bathrobe and watches us dabbing each other and close-talking and she shakes her head and wipes away a tear.

I'm just so happy, she says. I'm just just so happy to see you two back shooting buckets together. And I know Grandma would be so happy too, if only she could...

Damn, Auntie Shar, Swiss says turning his back on me. G'ma'd be too busy bitching at us to turn down the godforsaken gangster trash.

He says it the way Grandma said it. When my ma doesn't laugh he says it again even more accentuated: gangster traaash. Then he spits some tobacco juice on the gravel and digs it in with his foot.

He's standing between me and her, the garage light spilling out over his shoulder. His shadow dwarfing me on the driveway.

Sheet, yo, he says, looking back at me. Don't you remember, Cuz? Old G'ma was the biggest playa-hata there ever done was.

Yeah, I say. But bitch had her a good-ass heart.

In Our Defense We Didn't Set Out to Write a Pornographic Puppet Show

<u>1.</u>

It was 1993. It was a rural community in northern Wisconsin. Two of us were country kids, two of us small-town kids. Rich and Craig, being small-town kids, both had cable TV. Me and Danny being country kids did not.

<u>2.</u>

So far as I remember, the internet hadn't really been invented yet. Or maybe it had, but just not in northern Wisconsin. I didn't know anybody who had the internet. This includes my friends, my partners in crime.

<u>3.</u>

We were high school freshman. Craig being the oldest, having turned fourteen in August, me and Rich being the second and third oldest, having both turned fourteen in October. Danny was thirteen and would be until late April. At six-four he was by far the tallest and the only one who could grow respectable facial hair. Craig, meanwhile, had noticeable black arm and leg hair, but was far from jacked, and not sexy or manly in any particular way.

4.

Their names are not actually Danny, Rich, or Craig. I have changed the names to protect their identities. Everything else is true.

5.

Craig's father ran a funeral home. He was not a mortician. I don't know what his official title was but he ran the funeral home and handled all its business. I guess it would be funeral home director. Craig's father six foot five, with black bushy hair and black bushy mustache that made him look like a porn star from the seventies. He had been all-conference in basketball and football and spoke with a soft, slow, and baritone voice that came from deep in his very hairy chest which always sounded like he was about to break into *Fee fi fo fum… I smell the blood of an Englishman*. In some ways I imagine it must've been comforting to people mourning the loss of a loved one—in a James Earl Jones kind of way—but also highly intimidating when he would express his displeasure with you for being too loud, wild, or inappropriate at stayovers.

6.

Craig did not live at the funeral home, but sometimes we told others that he did by way of explanation why Craig was the way he was.

7.

I never really knew what Danny's dad did. Or mom. To be honest I don't even know if Danny's dad or mom got involved in any of this. As much as we hung out at school—took classes together, played sports together, cheated off each other's tests together—I can't ever remember hanging out at Danny's house or talking to Danny's parents. That's the kind of relationship we all had with Danny.

8.

Rich's dad was a plumber. It was a family business. Rich would one day take over the business and still runs it today.

9.

My mom was the home economics teacher and for reasons I never understood also taught seventh grade sex ed. It was a small school. All four of us had had my mom for sex ed. That is not a euphemism. However, Rich, Danny and Craig, along with most of my sixty-some classmates often used it as one. For example: *Yeah, I had Ben's mom for sex ed. Hasn't everybody had Ben's mom for sex ed?*

10.

We were all—even Craig—honor roll students, in the top twenty percent of our class. There were sixty kids in our class, but still. We all played multiple sports. We all participated in at least one other extra-curricular activity like FBLA or FHA. None of us at that time had ever even gotten so much as a detention. Teachers loved us. Coaches loved us. Parents loved us. Principal Cartright—not his real name—loved us. I don't think any of us at that time had ever had a drink of alcohol or a puff of a cigarette.

11.

In retrospect, Craig had probably drunk alcohol and/or a puffed a cigarette. Probably taken at least one hit of weed which may or may not have been his father's. This is not to point any blame in his direction.

12.

Of the four of us, none of us had had sex at that point. Except Craig.

13.

Once at a sleepover, Danny roughhoused a little too rough with Rich's Golden Retriever Goldie and got a boner and even more unfortunately he was wearing sweatpants so Craig, Rich, and I couldn't not see the huge tent sticking out from his sweatpants. This was further made awkward by the huge lipstick that Goldie was sporting. We didn't laugh or call it out at the time, but I am ashamed to admit that Craig, Rich, and I not only did not keep this a secret among the four of us, we also gave him the nickname DL which stuck with him at least until the day he graduated. DL for Daniel Lightner, but also, DL as in Dog Lover.

14.

I don't know if Rich ever kissed a girl in high school. I'm assuming he masturbated. I'm assuming that every boy in school probably masturbated, but it wasn't like he ever talked about it with us his closest friends or anyone else. He wasn't that type of kid. He wasn't Craig.

15.

By ninth grade, I had kissed two different girls, one in seventh grade and one in eighth grade. In a game of Truth of Dare at a co-ed stayover at Danny's house—his mom working an overnighter at the hospital—I had once touched Jenny Dewers's boobs under her bra. That was it for my sexual escapades. Sure, I masturbated, but only with my copy of the *Sports Illustrated Swimsuit Edition* with Kathy Ireland on the cover and not even with my hand which I didn't yet understand. Instead I would open the magazine to the foldout, put it on my pillow, and hump it until the pages got sticky or I ended up with a horrible papercut. In my defense, I didn't have an older brother, I had never seen a porno, never read any *Penthouse* letters, and as previously stated, we did not have the internet back then.

16.

For these and other reasons I remained virgin throughout high school. One of those other reasons being I had completely blocked out the trauma of my mother's sex ed class and thus had very little knowledge of the female anatomy. The only information I got was from Craig who told us all about the two holes. He called them the pee-hole and the vee-hole and he said you had to be careful not to put your dee in the pee-hole by accident because it could seriously hurt a girl and even give them an infection. Obviously, there was the bee-hole to consider as well, but he said some girls liked a little dee the bee-hole. And because we didn't have the internet for further research or clarification, the whole thing was quite intimidating to me. I know personally I never felt good about one-in-three odds. I'd played baseball my whole life and never hit .300, not even in tee-ball.

17.

Our teacher Mrs. Johnson—not her real name—was at least fifty years old, had long blond hair that often looked a little green, and wore short, tight, beige and other vaguely flesh-colored skirts and blousy semi-see-through shirts that showed off her freckled cleavage. In class she took turns sitting on different students' desktops while she read passages aloud from our essays during workshops.

What do we think of the author's intention here? she would say while sitting on the author-in-question's desk. What is he trying to tell us? The author not being permitted to speak until his piece had been workshopped by the class. The author having to sit there red-faced and try not to look at Mrs. Johnson's small but curvy butt on the desk in front of him while the entire class smirked and made many comments that could be construed as double-entendres.

18.

Mrs. Johnson believed in the value of daily journal writing. Sometimes it would be a reading response to whatever we had read for homework that day. Sometimes she would give us specific prompts that were supposed to help us practice whatever next essay we were to be writing, and sometimes we would do what Mrs. Johnson called *exquisite corpsing* where one person would write a line or two to a story/poem and then pass the journal to the person behind them who would then write another line or two adding to the story and so on and so on until you had close to a full page of a silly little story that didn't make much sense but was supposed to make writing fun and collaborative.

19.

I am not proud to admit this, but every time I got Danny's journal, whatever the line was before me, I would write, *Sadly, because Danny's such a dog lover, he's always had an easier time having relations with K9s than humankinds.*

20.

I'm pretty sure we'd learned that *having relations* meant *doing it* in Mrs. Johnson's class. I don't recall what story, poem, or play it would've been from but probably Shakespeare.

21.

Craig sat behind me in class and could never let it go when I'd write the line about Danny having relations with K9s. Craig sometimes let his creative juices get the best of him, and he could be quite descriptive in only a line or two.

22.

Until the whole children's puppet show fiasco, I don't think Mrs. Johnson ever read our journals closely. It was always check marks in the margins, maybe the occasional smiley face. A star at the top of the page to show we'd gotten full credit.

23.

I don't remember why Mrs. Johnson had us create our own puppet shows for children.

24.

I teach English now myself and I cannot imagine under any circumstances letting a bunch of horny high school students perform an un-vetted puppet show for elementary school students. But then again, I don't imagine she ever did again afterward either.

<u>25.</u>

It's not like I thought we were putting on *Sesame Street* or *Mr. Rogers Neighborhood*. Though it should be noted that a major character on Mr. Rogers Neighborhoods was named Mr. McFeely. I offer this only as cultural context of the bright-eyed, bushy-tailed world we grew up in.

<u>26.</u>

For obvious reasons, Craig volunteered to play the role of the Mighty Schlong Beast who he described as a cranky old dragon who spewed white lava whenever he got agitated. For obvious reasons, he said I would play the role of Chode Man who he described as a one-eyed flesh blob. He actually said that: *For obvious reasons* which meant he never actually explained why. For less obvious reasons Danny ended up playing Thumb Man and Rich ended up playing Pinky Girl.

<u>27.</u>

It's been twenty years now. I can't remember what Thumb Man was supposed to represent or if Pinky Girl actually had any sexual connotations or not. I wish I could recite some of the lines of dialogue or even a couple of the larger plot points. I can't. I can only remember that we did have a script and that we did perform this puppet show uninterrupted and uncensored for Mrs. Grabkowski's third grade class, including Mrs. Johnson's nephew Dylan—not his real name.

28.

I do remember the title: *Taming the Beast*.

29.

Mrs. Grabkowski's students all laughed, but not in an overly titillated way. They made oohing and ahing noises throughout our play, and based on this, I would argue they loved our play the best. Thankfully, the rest of our classmates waited out in the hall waiting for their turn and thus could not blow our cover.

30.

I could not bring myself to make eye contact with Mrs. Johnson throughout the performance, but Danny and Rich both did, and they said she seemed to really like it. She smiled and laughed at all the right parts and never once rolled her eyes or even frowned. But do you think she got it? I asked afterward out in the hall. I think she got it and I think she liked what she saw, Craig said. He still had his Mighty Schlong Beast puppet on his right hand and he was still talking in his low gravelly Sean Connery Schlong Beast voice. Christ, she's probably out there right now calling for an encore. Though I did not actually get *it* myself, I got *it* enough that I cringed at the thought and told Craig that was frickin gross. Mmm, speak for yourself Mr. Chode Man, he told me in his Sean Connery Schlong Beast voice. I'm just starting to get excited.

31.

If I blame anyone for this debacle, I do not blame Craig for leading us down this path. I blame Mrs. Johnson for assigning us the project in the first place and then for lying to us about our journals and I blame Mrs. Johnson's nephew Dylan for ratting us out to his cousin Drew who was sophomore and then Drew for ratting us out to his mother, Mrs. Johnson.

32.

When we got to class the next day at school, Mrs. Johnson slammed door in our faces. Or rather, she slammed Danny's forearm and knee in the door when Danny tried to block her from slamming the door in our faces. We'd been trying to beat the bell. She didn't bother asking if he was okay either. She just waited for him to step back and then she shut the door fully on us. And don't bother knocking until you're willing to admit what you did, she'd told us before she'd slammed the door on Danny. It wasn't as if she'd broken any of Danny's bones. But still, we brought up this act of violence many times over the course of the next week. She almost broke Danny's arm and knee, we'd say to anybody who'd listen.

33.

We sat out there the whole class and when we continued to play dumb, Mrs. Johnson said, Fine, we'll see what the principal has to say about it.

34.

Mr. Cartwright knew us well and often held us up as model students and scholar athletes and privately he told us he couldn't see anything inappropriate about Chode Man or Schlong Beast. He did admit that he could imagine someone misconstruing Mr. Thumb Man as related to masturbation, and though it was a bit more of a stretch, he could imagine how Mrs. Johnson might have read a little too much into the sexual connotations of Pinky Girl.

35.

When Principal Cartwright told Mrs. Johnson that he thought it was all just a big miscommunication, Mrs. Johnson said, Fine, let's see what their parents have to say this.

36.

When our parents came in to talk about the play, they all said they didn't see anything inappropriate with our puppet show. Including my mom who said quote-unquote: Well, I teach sex ed, and I've heard a lot of euphemisms in my time, but I'm not familiar with any of these. And Rich's dad who is a plumber who said quote-unquote: As a plumber, I think I've heard 'em all, and I ain't never heard of these.

37.

As stated earlier: I don't have any memory of Danny's mom or dad being at the meeting or having any involvement in this.

38.

Then there was Craig's dad who didn't say anything about running a funeral home or dealing with dead bodies. He gave a long hard look at Craig, sighed, and then back at the rest of us: Well, I can tell you this. My Craig knew full well what he was doing.

39.

I think maybe if it had just been the puppet show, we might've skated on it. But then to support her case, Mrs. Johnson offered into evidence the aforementioned journals. In one particularly racy entry, Craig had started an exquisite corpse about a kid named Danny who ran a dog grooming business named Danny's Doggy Styling. I don't think I have to spell it out what the gist of it was.

40.

Sure the journal was damning evidence to our past pornographic tendencies, but it also should've been inadmissible vis-à-vis Mrs. Johnson's stated policy that she would never show our journals to anyone else unless we were threatening to hurt ourselves or others. Our objections were overruled.

41.

Somehow we managed to avoid school suspension. I don't remember us even getting detention. This all seems wholly unbelievable now, especially within the world we live in these days where we probably would've been expelled and had our names broadcast across the internet news sites. But this was nearly thirty years ago. My best guess would be based on the fact that Principal Cartwright and the rest of our parents—excluding Craig's dad—still maintained that it was all an innocent mistake. Our only punishment: to redo our puppet show without any pornographic inuendo—to be viewed by Mrs. Johnson and Mr. Cartwright but no third graders.

42.

For some reason, with our second puppet show we decided to adapt the plot from Chicken Little. I think our thinking was that if it was already a children's story, we couldn't get in trouble. I also think it was a subtle jab at Mrs. Johnson for freaking out over an innocent little puppet show for third graders. *The Sky is Falling, the Sky is Falling.*

We did, however, make sure that Craig was not allowed to voice the character of Loosey Goosey.

43.

As far as I understand it, there is no hindsight exception to trial law. As far as I know you cannot use future suspicious acts to retry suspects for prior offenses.

44.

But the fact still remains: Two years later, a quiet student named Jamie Nelson who had a glass eye and worked as student janitor helper claimed that he walked in on Craig masturbating in the sink of the boys' bathroom after school. On one hand, it made no sense why Craig would be masturbating in the sink instead of doing it in the bathroom stall like everybody else and why not do it in the locker room if he was going to do it. On the other hand, none of us had ever heard Jamie Nelson speak more than ten words in a day and probably never told a dirty joke in his life. It was easiest to argue that Jamie had simply mistook what was happening rather than making it up completely, but it also always felt a little cruel to argue that One-Eyed Nelly—as students called him—hadn't *seen* it right.

45.

I wish I could say that Danny, Rich, and I stood up for Craig and declared his innocence. That we told everyone we knew that it was ridiculous and even as horny as Craig was, why would he be masturbating in a bathroom sink. Probably he'd just spilled something on the crotch of his pants—and yeah, maybe he had spilled that kind of something on his pants—but if he had, he'd've done it in the bathroom stall like a normal person and not have to get up on his tippy toes and somehow hoist up his leg just to get his junk close enough to shoot it all in there. I wish that I could say that Danny, Rich, and I didn't go around behind Craig's back saying things like *Yeah, I can believe it.* Or: *Sounds about right.* Or: *Dude is so fucked up, you should see what kind of kinky shit his dad is into, and he's a fucking mortician.*

46.

I wish I could say that Danny, Rich, and I didn't play a direct role in ruining Craig's remaining three years of high school. I always imagined that at some point before we graduated and left for college I would run into Craig at some party and apologize for turning us turning our backs on him when he needed it most.

47.

I don't remember ever talking to Craig about it. I don't remember us ever hanging out again. I haven't spoken to Craig or any of them in twenty years. We're not friends on social media.

48.

As far as I can tell, Craig is not currently in prison for any sexual offenses. Nor does he run a titty bar or a pornographic web site for sexual deviants. I looked it up. On the Internet. From his Facebook page, it appears that he is married with two kids and works as a ski instructor out in Vale, Colorado.

49.

My mom told me a couple years ago that Craig's father retired, sold his funeral home business, and moved away to be closer to his grandkids.

50.

It is hard, I'm sure, to look back on this and think we didn't know any better. But in our defense, I honestly don't think we did know better. Not even—no, *especially not*—Craig.

How He Did It

These days it's sorta like Choose Your Own Adventure, this game I play when I'm lying in bed trying to sleep. It's been twenty-five years since my big brother killed himself, and I still don't know how. I've been told. I've never asked.

So scenario one is always the old standby. Ray taking one of the old man's hunting rifles, sticking the barrel under the soft fleshy part of his jaw, and sitting at the foot of his bed.

Sometimes he uses the big toe. It's a tricky maneuver to pull off, if you think about it. Sometimes it's only the jagged edge of his right toenail, barely even a hangnail at most—to pull the trigger ever so gently and just that simply: Ka-blammo! A big mess of tongue, teeth, tonsils, and brain stem splattered all over the wall behind him like one of those Rorschach tests my old shrink used to make me take to prove I wasn't a threat to kill myself or others. As in, not like Ray.

This Rorschach, a big amorphous puddle of blood soaking into the shag carpeting underneath Ray's bed. A wiry pale naked chest and arms splayed out across the quilt atop his mattress.

This image of my dead brother is sometimes the only way I can pass out long enough to stop playing.

The problem with option one? I would've woken up. Wouldn't I? The blast of a hunting rifle, the thump

thump of a limp body hitting the floor. And me sleeping ten feet away in the next room.

So sometimes I'll try to forget all about my brother splattering his brains across the wall and choose another option. Maybe Ray taking the boxcutter out of his bedroom toolbox. Click, click, click! Then start carving out a big bloody Z for Zorro up and down and criss and cross his radial and ulnar arteries at the base of his wrist.

Why Z for Zorro? Because I've always imagined the Bat symbol would've been a bit too much blood and cutting. Even for somebody like Ray. For somebody like me to find, in real life or in my messed-up fantasies.

So instead I'd imagine a swift, quick, one-two-three on each wrist and then Ray holding up his hands in victory to let the blood drain more fluidly. Listen, I know it doesn't work that way. I know that real wrist-slitting takes more care and time.

What I wonder sometimes, Were you supposed to hold them down at your sides and make a fist to die more quickly? And would Ray've wanted quickly, or maybe to draw it out? So many questions I can only imagine the answers to.

There are other scenarios, of course.

Like the one out on the roof of our house. Atop the highest point, which just happened to be right above my bedroom window. Obviously I think I'd remember if he'd jumped from outside my window, but these years later I'm of a mind that I could probably forget just about anything if I try hard enough.

Like maybe Ray up there having stripped off all his clothes, the stance of an Olympic diver straddling the vee of the roof peaking just ten feet or so over the bed where I'm lying asleep, safe and sound.

Me, probably dreaming my little-kid dreams about G.I. Joe and all the Cobra guys shooting their little laser guns and all the G.I. Joes shooting their little laser guns back. Every soldier just letting loose with all their uzis and bazookas and M-16s and every other kind of big, badass gun they could bring to bear.

Everybody just raining down laser bullets on everybody else, and the whole while, no soldiers actually getting shot or even wounded, nobody actually getting blown up by enemy or friendly fire, or even dying any hideous bullet-ridden deaths at their own hands or the hands of the enemy.

And Ray, meanwhile, pointing his hands up above us head towards the skies, arching his back, getting one last good look at everything out there in the dark. Maybe saying one last little prayer for forgiveness. Maybe cursing all of us for letting him down.

Or maybe just getting his body aimed right, limbering up his legs and arms. Readying himself to both push off and let go.

Probably I'm in the middle of dreaming that I've saved the whole world again from imminent nuclear holocaust at the hands of Cobra and earning for my gallantry a smooch on the cheek from my pick of the hottest

G.I. Joe chicks around—Scarlet, of course. Scarlet planting a big wet one right on my heroic lips, maybe even slipping the tongue in there too.

The two of us playing major tonsil-hockey in front of the President of the United States, the Secretary of Defense, and all the other G.I. Joes, the full hero's treatment.

Me dreaming about my nightly missions all while Ray'd be perched naked to the night skies and ready to fly out into the darkness past my window.

And maybe I'd've been able to stop him. If only I'd woken up. If only I'd for real been out on one of my nightly missions, not dreaming away the nightly emissions. Ha! Get it?

I'd only later get the joke. Understand the difference between saving lives and wet dreams.

Ray probably shouting something all badass like Geronimo! or Timber! at the last second. The next two or three seconds it'd take to cover four stories. Would I have woken up in the process? Would I have heard the big splat-thump-thud right there in the middle of the concrete basketball court?

The basketball court where little pudgy ten-year-old me sometimes liked to take a break from my G.I. Joe missions just long enough to shoot a couple buckets, or until Ray'd make fun of me for always being such a fruity twink and for always playing such useless fruity twink games.

Hey Crusty, Ray'd always say. You gonna pull on your short-shorts and prance around with your bouncy balls?

Hey Crusty, Ray'd say sometimes after that. Check out my long-range game, and then see how far he could punt the basketball out into the woods behind the garage.

There are scenarios where there aren't any splattered brains or blood or chunks of hair and skin and internal organs to clean up off anything. One being just Ray, naked again, and this time having shaved his head.

Ray dangling some ten feet or so down from the roof of our old hayloft, the lasso looped up around the end of the hay elevator, the same lasso that a couple weeks before he'd done it, he'd used as a pulley system to hang that spotlight for me to be able to shoot buckets at night.

Ray's last gift to me. A big halogen lamp to light up that big empty hayloft at night. For me to shoot and shoot and shoot and try to forget about my being such a useless crybaby playing a fruity little game in the first place.

And Ray having gone and hung that lamp up there for me anyway, because he probably knew the whole time that he was gonna do it, and he wanted to give me some way to stop being such a pudgy little crybaby about everything and get up off my ass, out of the house, and toughen up a little bit.

Ha! I imagine Ray shouting down at me.

I imagine Ray dangling there naked in the middle of the hayloft with his freshly shaved head. You gonna catch me, Crusty? Smirking that shitty-ass smirk of his up above where the noose was cinched around his neck.

Hey Chicken Little, I imagine him taunting me. The sky is falling, the sky is falling.

Ray's pale wiry puppet body suddenly come back to life to mock me.

The sky is falling, Crusty! I'd imagine Ray mocking me in his highest-pitched crybaby voice. The sky is falling. Save me, Crusty. Save me.

Then waving his arms and legs around in the air, the squeak and clank of the hay elevator straining under Ray's weight as he swings from one side of the barn to the other.

Catch me, Crusty, I imagine Ray saying as I stab at the air for something to grab. Catch me, I'm dying here.

Ray's eyes bugging out and then rolling back in his head, his voice growing even more strained as he'd shout, I'm gagging, Crusty, I'm choking! Can't you see that, you little crybaby? Can't you catch me? Can't you come to my rescue, Crusty? Can't you save me with all those G.I. Joe dolls you're always playing with? Can't you for, God's sake, get me down before I choke, Crusty?

Ah, Christ, I imagine Ray saying eventually, Are you crying again, Crusty? Is wittle crybaby Crusty gonna run and tell Mommy that big bad Ray was being mean to him again?

And then I imagine Ray's body going limp and just hanging there once again in my mind. Naked except for the noose around his neck.

Not that any of these dreams are true. These dreams that aren't even dreams. They're the masochistic scenarios that run through my mind while I'm trying to get to the dreams. And to the sleep.

Twenty-five years, and I'm still running through scenarios in my head of how my brother killed himself less than ten feet away from where I would've been sleeping in the next room.

The only option I can truly remember is the one where I remember nothing until long afterward. The one where I'm talking to a female cop later that night, all the questions she'd asked.

Did you hear anything? she asked.

Had you talked to your brother much over the last couple days? she asked.

Had he said anything or done anything odd? she asked.

Odd? I wanted to ask her. What's odd at this point? And how would I know the difference?

The TV had been playing in the background with the sound turned down, that's what I remember. Some infomercial for that ThighMaster thing where you stuck this rap-trap-looking contraption between your legs and smiled at everybody while you squeezed your knees shut.

Had I noticed anything different about Ray's behavior over the last few weeks? This cop with her gut—sometimes I remember her pregnant, other times just fat—how it'd blocked my view of all those chicks squeezing their knees together and smiling their big shiny smiles at me.

Odd behavior? I often still think to myself. Was it odd to watch beautiful women work their ThighMasters only hours after your brother had killed himself?

Or what about that last week when Ray'd put up a light in the barn so I could shoot baskets at night? How much Ray had hated basketball and teased me about basketball and still he'd put it up for me?

Was that odd?

Or how about afterward when Ray'd just hung there upside down with his knees over the hay elevator? How about when Ray kept on asking if I was gonna catch him if he fell.

Was that odd behavior? I want to go back and ask that cop. Or was it just typical big brother stuff? Boys will be boys and such.

The thing is, I don't remember any answers I gave or could've given. I remember only the questions and the things I could've said but didn't, or maybe just the things I want to have said in my own ten-year-old defense.

Because that's the thing with time and memories, the more you play them out in your head, the more time goes by, the more you start to play what-if and Choose Your Own Adventure. The more they start to take on a narrative of their own.

Maybe I told that lady cop all about the light in the barn and Ray hanging by his feet. Maybe I told that lady cop about the way Ray would sometimes pounce on me when we were younger. Pin me down and pound my nuts trying to make a man of me.

Stop crying, he'd always say as he pinned me down. Stop crying, Crusty, or I'll give you something to cry about.

Maybe I told that lady cop about all my G.I. Joe dreams and my nightly missions to save the day. My nightly emissions. Was that odd? On the night my brother killed himself?

Or maybe I told that cop nothing. Maybe I just sat there and sniffle and sobbed and shook my head.

No, I can't think of anything odd that Ray's ever said or done to me. It was all typical big brother/little brother stuff.

Even this, I maybe told that cop: Well, officer, whichever way he'd killed himself, it was classic Ray. Just the type of thing a big brother would do to get the last laugh on his whiney, crybaby brother.

It was like he was saying, Quit your crying, Crusty, or I'll give you something to cry about.

It was like saying, The sky is falling, the sky is falling. And you're gonna save me?

How Ray did it? What I do remember about that night or the weeks leading up to it? What he'd said and what he'd done. Twenty-five years. All the possible scenarios. Who could even say what had or hadn't happened anymore?

Was that odd?

A Good Ram Is Hard to Find

Poetry

Dude types it big and bold, all caps atop a blank page. *DEAR DEAD MAMA.* Slams the carriage return on his dead mother's old Smith-Corona. Listens for the ding. Feels for the ding. Dude kind of lovin' that ding. The sound of starting again.

It's near dawn, end of November. Thanksgiving come and gone. Dude living back home with his old man out in the barrens of Bumbfuck Nowhere, about as far the fuck north in Wisconsin as you can get without drowning in Lake Superior. Wind colder than a witch's tit, coming off the shore. Dude holed up in the attic of his parents' farmhouse, no Internet, no computer, not a goddamn cell phone to text on.

Dude and his hairy little middle fingers spastically pecking away. All three hundred pounds of Dude stripped bare save for a threadbare pair of Hanes hanging on to their seams for dear life. Dude sweating balls, the radiator clanking and whining along the carpeted floor near his rotten-ass feet. Dude tryin' his damnedest to block everything out and write his ma a suitable ode.

Everything fuckin' dead or dyin', Ma. / And here I am, Ma, ya' baby boy / all grown up and tryin' to write somethin' nice.

Where all your imagery when I need it, Ma? / All that pretty pretty goddamn poetry / you always said would save me?

Dude sniffling a little, wiping his nose on his sweaty shoulder. Eyes welling up as he stares off into the closet doors he's boarded up over the windows. Dude humming the tune of his favorite Eminem song: *I'm sorry Mama / I never meant to hurt you / I never meant to make you cry but tonight / I'm cleanin' out my closets.*

Can you hear that music? Dude's mother used to whisper in his ear. *Can you hear your muse calling to you?*

Dude, four, five, six, seven years old pudgy as shit, propped up on his old lady's lap and learning to write his little kid pomes. The way she'd grab his little fingers off the keys and make him tap-tap-tap on the open window next to them. *Whatever words you're trying to find, baby, all you need is a clear mind and an open window. Listen closely enough and eventually your muse will sing to you.*

Dude now a grown-ass man-baby, thirty-three years old like fuckin Jesus, who went and martyred himself just to save the souls of pathetic degenerate losers like dude, an out of work high school janitor. Couldn't even follow in his old man's custodial footsteps, the job his old man had to pull strings to get his deadbeat son in the first place.

What kind of dude gets fired from scrubbing shitters? This dude. Sweating and sniveling, sitting there in those dirty undies, staring at a few puny pathetic rhymes, all that blank page. Dude squirming a little from cheek to cheek, adjusting the bunch sticking up his ass crack, in the process accidentally letting loose a little quacker.

Ah shit Ma, he mutters. *See what you do to me?*

He sniffles again, then props his other cheek and lets out another, this one silent but deadly. *Can you feel the breeze, Ma? / Can you smell my imagery?*

But where's the poetry? his ma used to ask him back when he'd show her all little white boy wannabe rap pomes. Dude, thirteen, fourteen, fifteen, and all his pomes filled with *bitches* and *big tits* and *badass motherfuckers with huge dicks.*

Dude's old lady shaking her head and holding her heart. Tsk-tsk-tsking at what had happened to everything she'd taught him. What had happened to that window into her baby-boy's sweet little poet heart?

Yo, Ma, Dude typing, *it's already six in the mornin' / and where's your goddamn sun / stretchin' out its shinin' arms across horizon?*

Where all your chirpy-ass little chickadees singin' their goddamn mornin' songs? / Your larks / your cardinals / your mourning doves / and mockingbirds?

Where all your foxes at, your deer, your rabbits, your squirrels, Ma? / It's still dark out and no sign of no raccoons, stray cats, no bats / not one goddamn possum? I can't hear no chickens, no geese, no sheep, no bellowin' cows?

I can't hear your fuckin' muse, Ma? Can you?

Po-ems, what dude's ma used call them, his silly little rap pomes. *Tsk-tsk-tsk,* she'd say and hand him his songs back covered in red. *To be honest, these all make me a little sad,* she'd tell him, shaking her head. *You keep trying so stubbornly to make all this ugliness rhyme, your po-ems have completely lost any sense of po-etry.*

Dude really getting his panties in a twist just thinking about all his ma's guilt and disappointment. Ain't even his own panties riding up his swampy ass crack, but rather the granny panties of his dead mother's. Laundry day for weeks now, but that ain't even it. Dude's pathetic degenerate's attempt to find a new muse from something old and used. That pile of all her delicates he's been putting off dealing with, the damp and dank stink lingering from sitting a month atop the washer down in the basement. Dude scrunching up his nose and closing his eyes as he scrounged and scrounged 'til he'd found the cleanest dirty pair of her granny panties that he was going to find.

What was Dude supposed to do with the dirty laundry of dead loved one? Donate them to the homeless? Throw them out with the rotten kitchen scraps, microwave dinner containers, and stale beer cans? Burn them in effigy? Or seek in them the fucked-up inspiration to write one last love pome to the only one who'd ever believed in him, the woman, who after thirty years of disappointing her, he'd finally done gone and broken her heart?

Dear dead Mama, please forgive your me, Dude starts again. He's mouthing the words while he pecks the words one letter at a time. *Ya'boy didn't mean to break your heart, see? / He just couldn't grow up to be the pretty boy poet you always wanted him to be.*

Boy. What Dude's old man still calls him. *As in when you gonna quit messin' around with those goddamn and get yourself a job, boy?*

A Good Ram Is Hard to Find

Boy? The old man's up and at 'em and already nagging on him. The old man garbling and hacking and probably drooling, too, at the foot of the stairs.

But dude's too caught up in the zone to listen to no one trying to break his flow.

Why why why, me of my, Ma / Why'd you have to go and die die die? / Why why why when I'm the one deserves to die?

There's a creak at the bottom of the stairs, the clunk-clunk of the railing's screws loose against the drywall. Another thing dude hasn't gotten around to doing since he'd moved back home.

You tryin' to kill me, boy? the old man's voice unsteady from the second step to the third.

Dude's stubby middle fingers flying fast as he can mouth the rhymes spilling out his head. *Can't you hear me cryin? / Can't you see me up here tryin'? / Can't you even appreciate this goddamn love pome I'm writin'?*

There's the thump-slide-thumping with each step the old man takes, his bad hips, bum knee, etcetera etcetera. *You hear me, boy?*

But of course boy can't hear him. Boy is Dude this morning, and all Dude can hear are his mad rhymes and all his ma guilt and nagging: *But what about the imagery? What about the poetry? Can't you this one time write your dear mother something that isn't so ugly?*

Do you want to hear about the soft sad cooing of the mourning doves? dude writes/raps/pleads with his dead mother. *Is that the type of beautiful shit you want to hear me?* Dude all but shouting now in time to his typing. *Or how about those annoying-ass mockingbirds? All their shitty chirp-chirp-chirping in my ear?*

Dude's old man, stooped over outside the door now, his pitted-out v-neck t-shirt, his black compression socks up to his knees, no pants on, sure, but his own set of stretched out tighty whiteys. As in *for men*—not boys, not grannies, not dead women.

Boy, he says again, the old man banging down the locked door of his dead wife's writing room. *What'd I tell you about lockin' yourself up in your ma's office all night?*

And: *That's your mother's office, ya' know? Ain't your playroom.*

And: *What you think your mother would say about you in there alone all night doin' God knows what?* What would Dude's mother say?

She'd be saying what she'd always been saying: *Where's my motherfuckin' poetry?*

Or rather, she'd be saying: *My prodigy, my one and only son, all these rhymes and you can't write one image save your mother's soul.*

She'd be saying: *Oh my broken, broken heart how it bleeds. Can't you be bothered to write me one poem about love and beauty?*

Dude thinking so loud he can't hear the old man's arthritic hands twisting the doorknob this way and that, the ting-ting-ting of his pocketknife picking at the lock.

Dude doing his best to let the sound of each syllable he spits drown out all the shame and self-doubt. *Dear dead*

A Good Ram Is Hard to Find

Mama, he types, *I'm tryin' so hard to find the words but still I can't hear you? / Dear dead Mama, the window's open and my mind's clear / but here I am again locked up all alone / tryin to write you one last poem you can be proud of.*

Dude so caught up in his emotions he's about to jump fat ass out of his chair and tear down the closet doors. Open the window and let the rising sun creep in. But that's when he finally hears the lock click, the hinges creek, the thump-slide-thump of his old man one foot in the door and about to have himself a stroke.

Dude's finally got himself an image: the old man squinting at first, blinking out the light spots against a hazy lamp in the corner. His brown eyes eventually opening wide and watery, what must be the slow fading away of the fuzziness around the flushed pasty blob of his only son on full display, or nearly full.

Dude wondering how long it might take for his old man to recognize his dead wife's underwear. Or if he'd be able to make them out at all, his mother's undersized panties dwarfed by his son's distended belly, stretch marks, and spare tire.

The old man old man mumbling for a beat, then making a sucking sound, a groan, and grasping at his chest while collapsing to the ground.

What's wrong, Dad? Dude asking, like, honestly he doesn't know damn well what's been coming, what he's done to his old man this time. *What's wrong, Dad!*

Dude at some point running over to straddle his old man's hairy legs. Dude and his dad suddenly pressed up crotch to crotch, undies to undies. Dude pumping and pumping away on his old man's brittle chest.

Dad, Dad, Dad? Dude keeps saying, keeps pumping, keeps slapping the old man gently across the face.

And what an image they were, Dude can't help but think. What a final turn to Dude's pome. The two men's bodies convulsing, top and bottom. Their mouths now conjoined, the chapped lips and sandpaper stubble. All that steam against the early morning light slipping in through the door like a halo. All that heat suddenly between them, suction and slobber. The depth of old man's windpipe going on and on forever, no bottom. Dude wheezing and sobbing and sucking wind in between blowing his lungs out. All the while Dude writing a another new pome, this one for his father:

Dad, Dad, Dad! / Don't die, Dad! / Dad don't die.

Don't you fuckin' die on me now, Dad. / Don't you fuckin' abandon me, too.

The girth of Dude's love and shame collapsing over his old man's quivering body. Maybe this was his mother's muse finally speaking to him, an open window, the image he'd always been missing. He and his old man engulfed in their own love and grief. Dude finally listening to his beating heart.

My Childhood PTSD as Triggered by the Following Movie Montage

I. That scene in *American History X*, y'all know it. The curb. The stomp. Or maybe it was *Higher Learning*, I always get those confused. I once face-planted in the barn while corralling bull calves, to get castrated, my two front teeth chomping down on all that jagged concrete and manure, it adds a different flavor to the recurring nightmare I have, though in my case, usually nothing to do with race relations. I wonder if everybody else who watched that movie also missed the whole point of it. Except the Curb Stomp. Everybody remembers where they were when their stoner friend with big ideas about ending racism across the world made them watch the movie with the Curb Stomp.

II. Mel Gibson getting drawn and quartered. You may take our lives, but you will never take... our... FREE-DOM!

III. Mel Gibson ripping his shoulder out of its socket in *Lethal Weapon*.

IV. Mel Gibson torturing the shit out of Jesus, blaming the women and Jews for everything, including his drunk-driving and plummeting career options.

V. Any movie where somebody's sitting there reading a book before bed, watching TV, gossiping with girlfriends, when the camera pulls back only to zoom back in on the dark night window behind them—cue the string section.

VI. Mostly I'm thinking of that one zombie movie, something *28 Days* something, but not the one about Sandra Bullock finding love with Viggo in rehab. It's not even about the zombies. It's about the dark night window, not to be confused with the Dark Knight window, sorry that was shitty of me. But the secluded house. I grew up in a big old farmhouse out in the barrens of northern Wisconsin. Lots of windows, no shades. In so many ways I grew up in the dark. It wasn't the zombies I worried about. It was the meth heads. Which, sure, I guess if you're getting technical about it, same thing, fine, you win, I'm scared of zombies.

VII. That part of that one weird depressing Robin Williams's movie with Robin Williams's kids get killed in a car accident while backing out of the driveway on the way to school. The one where Robin Williams later on gets plowed over by a truck going the wrong way while out trying to help another couple who'd been injured in a different car accident, but before all that his wife kills herself because she can't take it and then Robin Williams goes to the suicide afterlife to save her and fucking Cuba Gooding Jr. who—spoiler alert—turns out to be the ghost/angel of his dead son explaining to Robin Williams that his wife/his mother can't be saved because she killed herself, it doesn't matter that she had a pretty fucking good reason too, she's still stuck face down floating around in that black swamp of bodies of everybody else's killed themselves and nobody's getting to heaven. [quote about I'm not going back] That shit really messed me up, not the car accidents, the afterlife for selfish losers like me who kill themselves.

VIII. The Zapruder film, but as replayed by Kevin Costner in Oliver Stone's fever dream of a conspiracy theory, the magic bullet, back and to the left, back and to the left, back and to the left. How it gets stuck in my head, JFK's exploding head replaced with my brother's exploding head, sometimes my own, except unlike my brother and JFK my head's still mostly intact. Back and to the left, back and to the left. Sometimes I think about that too with that one *Seinfeld* episode with Keith Hernandez and the magic loogie, but usually the loogie gets replaced with a bullet and Kramer's head gets replaced with my brother, mine, back and to the left.

IX. The sound of the gun shots in the final scene of that Tom Hanks movie where he plays himself again, a good guy, a family guy, a sly sense of humor, but this time a mob hitman with a strained relationship with his oldest son. The look on Tom Hanks's face walking back to the house from the ocean—having survived it all, the hit that his old mob bosses had put out on him for putting a hit on his old mob boss's son—one of them being James Bond, the other being [old guy]. The other one being that one guy with his eye shot out. But this is all past all that, it's the happy ending. They're on a beach somewhere, white sand, somebody's house that Tom Hanks and his kid are going to live in now. The silence before and after. Jude Law! It's Jude Law's face, his eye all fucked up, how did it happen, I don't really remember the specifics but I remember the specifics.

Bang, bang, bang. I think it might've had something to do with Jude Law being a photographer, like one of those where you pose with your kid or something or say you get promoted to head CEO or godfather of the family. Smile. Click, click.

X. The gunshot at the end of *American Beauty*, pretty much the same thing, different movie. Chris Cooper confusing Kevin Spacey as gay but before Kevin Spacey actually came out as gay, and a sexual predator. Both in the movie in real life, well not really, but sorta. You get the point.

XI. Jared Leto as Angel Face getting his face punched in by Ed Norton as Brad Pitt as Tyler Durdin's split personality in *Fight Club*. Not so much Jared Leto, but the wet mushy sounds of it. That part on the audio commentary where Chuck Palahniuk and David Fincher defend the violence of the movie, Fincher pointing out that he was not glorifying violence, he was making it realistic. That's what it sounds like to punch your opponent into the concrete, Fincher says and Palahniuk laughs and agrees. Don't worry, I'm not going to make any puns about the first rule of fight club.

XII. *Requiem for a Dream*, the entirety of it, but everything else I've blacked out now with years of never shooting up myself or watching my friends shoot up. Only a random jump cut that pops up in my consciousness at random intervals: a close-up of a girl shooting up, or being shot up, everything else in the room gone blurry, whatever ambient music they're playing.

XIII. The bulging vein in Tom Cruise's head from *Magnolia*. Respect the Cock and Tame the Pussy, Respect the Cock and Tame the Pussy. I think probably my therapist would have some thoughts about all this, and some questions. Questions and thoughts.

XIV. That one version of a *Christmas Carol* when the Ghost of Christmas Past with the alien children living under his robe.

XV. I once got the worst set of blue balls you could imagine while taking my best friend's girlfriend to Baz Lurman's remake of *Romeo and Juliet*. That *Romeo and Juliet*. I missed most of it, I kept having to go to the bathroom to masturbate in agony and to no avail. Leo and Claire Danes are hot and heavy on an acid trip, and every time my best friend's girlfriend reaches for a handful of popcorn she makes sure to wipe the butter off on the inside of my upper thigh. This is what I get for being the good guy of falling on the grenade for my best friend, the grenade in this case being Shakespeare and my best friend's hatred of literature.

XVI. Mark Wahlberg's flaccid rotten dick in *Boogie Nights*.

XVII. *The Secret of the Crying Game*, but not in a transphobic kind of way. The smallness of it is what gets me. The tenderness. The growing tent in my pants at its sudden appearance on the screen. You won't believe this but I was a naïve, podunk kid from off the farm, I didn't have cable, I didn't have access to the internet. His/her secret opened up a lot of questions for me. I often dream of dressing up in drag and someone sucking my little bitty dick and if that makes me a little bit gay or maybe bi or what's it called, body dysmorphic. I mean I guess it doesn't matter anymore, it's the new millennium, we're all a bit sexually confused, aren't we?

XVIII. This one porno my friends and I watched at somebody's uncle's cabin up in the UP for a three-on-three basketball tournament. *The Snapping Pussy*. The sound her vagina made, like somebody really dramatic at clicking their tongue and slurping a half-empty malt the same time. The scene of us boys all sitting there with our boners watching a porn and wanting to masturbate but not because we were all boys and we were afraid we'd be gay. Not that there's anything wrong with being a little bit gay.

XIX. A made-for-TV movie as best as I can remember, me six, seven years old and home alone while my big brother, supposed to've been baby-sitting me, the only time he ever babysat me, which he didn't, he went out to a party, the movie about some kid who'd watched his mother get murdered, and then goes mute, keeps drawing these pictures of Peter Pan and Captain Hook. The kid's grandfather, one of those big hooks, like the one in *I Know What You Did Last Summer*, but this was long before that, though I'm not sure it was before the book. Did you know that there was a book *I Know What You Did Last Summer*? I mean this isn't about the book or the movie, this is about that kid whose grandfather gutted his own daughter who'd he'd molested for years with a fishhook and then how he'd then comeback to finish the job with his mute grandkid, I don't know how this movie ever got green-lighted (green-lit?) for TV, but then it's weird to even think about those made-for-TV movies and if they actually existed or if I'm just making this whole thing up, but then my brother, we'd had a walk-in basement at the time, this being before I'd accidently burned that house down with two space heaters stolen from the barn, before my brother'd killed himself, he'd come back late, or probably it was only eight or nine, but I was young and alone out in the woods where we lived, and he'd come back through the basement, which was attached to the family room, where I'd been watching and then *all of a sudden* that kid on TV was being stocked by his granddad with a fish hook and the door to the basement was opening, and for god knows why I'd turned off all the lights to watch the scary movie by myself, and it turns out it was just my brother who'd end up killing himself in like a year, maybe six months, and he was just playing a little prank on me, or maybe he'd just come through the basement for some reason, he was always hanging out down there and tinkering around with things, but in my mind, I can remember that exact look on his face, that smirk, even in the dark, the light from the television in a blacked-out room, a blacked out house, reflecting off those pop-bottle glasses of his, the shiny too-big-for-his-face silver frames. My mother always tells me I should try to remember the happy times I had with my brother, and honestly, I can't, I can only remember that smirk, those glasses, the handle turning a moment before he appeared.

XX. Any and all sequels where it turns out that the dead character didn't actually die at all, or maybe it's magic, or maybe there's time travel.

XXI. Any happy ending ever.

XXII. Every ending in my worst nightmares involves everyone I've ever loved and hated turning to snake heads. Snakeheads, snake arms, snake butts. Snakes, snakes, snakes. They slip out of their clothes and come up from under my bed, slither under my covers. They bite me, they kiss me, poison me, they consume me whole and regurgitate my bones. That's how they always end. Me dead and abandoned.

XXIII. That scene in the first Indiana Jones with Indiana Jones and getting trapped in the cave with all the snakes. I hate snakes. All my worst nightmares turn to snakes. Fuck snakes. This all might have something to do with my undersized penis. If you want to go down that path. *The Secret of My Crying Game.*

A Good Ram Is Hard to Find

Jonesing for Jesus

I already know Nurse Nancy in ways I shouldn't and now she's probably told Dr. Van Penis, which may or may not be his real name but sounded true when it rolled off Nurse Nancy's voluptuous lips, and for all I know they're both conspiring to have me signed off to a padded room and for nothing more than a small finishing nail impaling the palm of my hand. Nurse Nancy is tsk-tsk-tsking me while she cleans my gaping wound tenderly. Oh my, she says and purses those lips inches from my drooling mouth. Says Uffda that's a nasty little owie you've gone and given yourself this time. Calls me Sweetie like always.

What the doctor who may or may not have a huge wang may not know is Nurse Nancy is not this Mother Theresa she'd have us all believe she is.

Two months earlier it was the same routine and shaking her head, as she stared at the jagged line of puckered stitches running down my wrists. Uffda, she was saying again. And then: What oh what are we gonna do with you, Sweetie?

But two nights later, I'm rubbing cocoa butter all over the glorious stretchmarks mapping the path of my fingers across thighs and calves, belly and back, all that hot doughy flesh! Giving her the old one-handed naked massage.

Maybe I shoulda known better, but Nurse Nancy looked, and still looks tonight, like a Barbie Doll, except pasty and bloated, like Barbie moved to Minnesota and got an allergic reaction from eating too much hotdish and lefsa. And I get this jones for the ones where they're round and squishy, ripping out of their clothes in the all the right places. The Incredible Hulk two seconds before David Banner turns into Lou Ferigno. But female.

Anyway, I can smell the cocoa butter on Nurse Nancy's skin as she's a' pump-pumping away on her blood pressure pump, squeezing the pale, blue life out of my quivering arm. She knows I smell it, too, but she's waiting for me to get down and grovel.

Says I'm one-ninety-eight over eighty-seven. Too high, Sweetie. She sighs and shakes her head at me. Those big brown eyes of hers tell me I need to quit all these shenanigans or I'm gonna get a heart attack and drop dead behind the next dumpster I fall in love with. The strays are gonna piss on my corpse, her sigh tells me, and the cops are gonna leave me there to make wingless snow angels on the cracked pavement of some lonely back alley.

She says the doctor will be with me shortly. The woman's used that lie to placate me three times now.

I can hear Dr. Van Penis—and yes, now I think that may be his God-given name—working over some old man in the adjacent curtain. What sounds to be a fractured hip while trying to cane away from his eldest son. The old man is telling Dr. Van Penis that his son is a dirty Jew. That his son's always trying to Jew him out of his retirement and stick him in a home. That he should've never married a damn Jew and had Jew kids in the first place, that this is what he gets for marrying into a people who would sacrifice a perfectly nice possible messiah out of nothing more than petty jealousy.

What about that guy? I'm asking. And why am I the sick one?

Tsk-tsk-tsk, Nurse Nancy says and tells me again that Dr. Van Penis will be with me in a moment. The way she keeps saying his name tells me she wants me to know how big his dick is, the things she could do with it if she wanted to, right here in front of me and my gaping wound. Her tone says, Now how would that make you feel, Mister?

I may be attributing too much to the tone of her voice.

The night after I had allowed her to smother me with her considerable healing powers, I went and called up her seventeen-year-old daughter, Alice, who lives with her. She wasn't quite as buxom and fully matured in the bust the way her mother was and is and forever will be, but I went ahead and let her try to save me with her own amateur remedies. In my defense, I had been calling for the adult version. But the girl had picked up and told me she'd committed a terrible sin and if I came over and prayed with her, she'd suck on my John the Baptist as if it were oozing with Jesus's forgiveness. Alice may not be entirely right in the head, but then again, I am not entirely a healthy man.

Most times my jonesing can be quenched with small sacraments — putting out cigarettes on my forearm, holding a zippo under my wrist until I peel off a skin portrait of the Virgin Mary. The usual sacrifices—nothing worth a special trip to confession.

And just try answering honestly to the Lord: Dear Jesus, forgive me, but I may be afflicted with what you would call a masochistic fix for Your love. And sometimes in my sinful desires I get a jonesing to crucify my palms with Your love, dear Jesus. To purge the sin from my ever-loving appendages—usually my left because as You have taught me, dear Jesus, left means sinister and sinister appendages mean sinful deeds. So if I have impaled myself with a nail gun again, it was not that I was questioning the gift of life—Your greatest gift, Dear Jesus! What it was purifying my nasty parts, so their sins might be forgiven. Forgiven by you, my Lord.

Nurse Nancy comes back to my curtain to usher in Dr. Van Penis and tells me not to worry. Dr. Van Penis is going to fix me up in a jiffy and then these nice young men—the doctor's got two strapping male nurses to support him—they're going to help me stop hurting myself. According to the woman who wants to condemn me to eternal damnation for past transgressions.

Of course, Nurse Nancy has gone and had her cake and eaten it too. I might as well be down on my knees begging for forgiveness. She knows it, I know it, but how about Dr. Big Dick or his gay henchmen disguised as nurses? Is everybody in cahoots?

Well, I do the only thing that comes to mind. I hold up three fingers and all that blood that's come back alive running down my wrist, my forearm, the side of my wife-beater. How there, kemosabes, I say. I'm up off my gurney now to show I'm fit and fiddle.

Where you think you're going, Sweetie? Nurse Nancy says.

But I'm done talking to her. I'm looking for converts now. You must forgive Mr. Lefty, I say. Just so everybody's clear on the issue at hand, I'm pointing straight at the nail impaling the intersection of my lifelines. I can feel the tickle of each drop of blood as it drips off the tip of my elbow and onto my shirt, my shoes, the floor.

Dr. Van Penis is wide-eyed with one hand clasped over his mouth, aghast. The other clenching those latex gloves he's prematurely taken out of the box. He's exchanging glances with his henchmen, then Nurse Nancy, then the crinkled place on the gurney paper where they all think I should still be sitting.

Oh Sweetie, Nurse Nancy says, you shouldn't be waving that thing around like that. You're gonna do some serious nerve damage.

Mr. Lefty, I say, turning my punctured hand, like a talking puppet, to Dr. Van Penis. He wrong this nice nurse lady here, I say, turning my hand to the male nurses. He think sinister thoughts about healing women folk sometimes, I say, turning my hand back to myself. He try to purify too much. I'm shaking my head and shunning my punctured hand for extra emphasis.

Sweetie, why don't you just sit back down there on the white paper and let the doctor and these nice men have a look at that booboo you got there.

You no worry now, Lady, I say. I'm trying not to get distracted by the trail of blood I'm leaving with my hand puppet. Me teach him *strong* lesson—yes?

Not one of these guys with balls enough to even nod back at me, let alone my bloody hand. With nail gun—yes?

Sweetie? She's got me by my good one now, her sausage fingers so warm and moist against the inside of my good wrist. She's got those two fertile crescents of hers to herd me back towards the gurney.

But he no sinister no more, I say over my shoulder. Me purge him of sin. I'm looking for any opening, I'm waiting for someone to part the seas. See? I tell Nurse Nancy. See? I tell the doctor with the big dick, the nurses with their blank faces and folded arms.

But Nurse Nancy has me secured snugly in her clutches once again. She's trying to smother me with her overwhelming forgiveness. She's saying everything's going to be okay. Saying the good doctor and these nice strapping young men here are going to help me help myself. She says it's all for the best. She's pinning me down now. None of the men seem to be doing anything to help.

But can't you see? I shout over her vast chest, her meaty shoulders. I'm healed, I shout. I'm healed, can't you see?

A Good Ram Is Hard to Find

Work

50

This being a Tuesday. I remember because it'd been the morning after *Raw*'d had to go and cancel the kayfabe funeral service they'd planned for Mr. McMahon that night.

In its place a real tribute to Chris Benoit, aka the Crippler, or sometimes the Canadian Crippler, and occasionally just the Rabid Wolverine. He'd gone and choked himself to death sometime over the weekend. Bodies of him and his wife and kid being discovered that afternoon a few hours before McMahon's funeral'd been set to air.

Uncle Rog's reading all about it in paper behind me, while I'm flipping eggs and trying fill in all the stuff the news always leaves out. Pretty much all the important shit.

For example, shoot is what they call it when reality starts getting in the way of a work. Or sometimes they have what they call a worked-shoot, which is where everything gets a little confusing.

Like how all the wrestlers'd had to break kayfabe for the night to talk about what a great guy the Crippler'd been. Real wrestlers' wrestler. Consummate professional. Never no-showing. Never taking unnecessary risks. Always protecting guys from getting hurt.

Yah, real hero, Rog says. He's got the paper laid out across the cutting board. Tracing the words with the tip of this eight-inch carving knife. The way he's got that carving knife in his hand pretty much every hour of every day of every shift I've ever worked with him.

49

Maybe top five wrestling technicians of all time. What CM Punk says.

Weeks earlier, Benoit's bashing the guy's head in with a steal chair, getting disqualified. He's locking that Crossface in good and tight, almost snapping the guy's neck in two. Not letting up no matter how many times the ref calls for the bell.

What they always say in wrestling: steal chair. Never: folding chair. Never just: chair. Always: *steal* chair.

Then suddenly the Crippler's dead. Nobody knows why, nobody knows how, and Punk's breaking down blubbering about what a loss it is. What a terrible, tragic, senseless loss it is. For everybody.

Of course, the details being a little fuzzy at that point. As of when they go on air that night, the police haven't released much more than the name: Chris Benoit, professional wrestler, wife, and son.

By this morning the papers are saying Benoit'd choked himself to death, but only after first putting the Crippler Crossface on his wife then kid. Strangulation, the police call it. What Rog is underlining with the tip of his carving knife. What Rog is huffing and puffing about.

Whether you find this all fitting or just ironic, I say, probably a matter of perspective.

48

First day I ever worked here, Rog's reading the paper with that knife as his place holder same as this morning, same as every morning he preps for lunch and dinner.

So I walk up from behind him to introduce myself. Mumble: Hey, I'm the new breakfast guy.

He snaps around on me, sticks that thing an inch from my jugular, says, You wanna get stabbed, kid? You got a death wish? That it?

Son, in this kitchen you don't never walk behind a man with a knife in his hands unless you ready to die. You hear me?

Same thing at least once a week for all the years I been here: walk behind him, don't say nothing. Mind my own business. Only to have that psycho spin around and stick that thing in my face. You gotta death wish, boy? You wanna get stabbed?

Cut your goddamned tongue out, maybe you speak up then, eh?

47

Anyway, best friend a guy could ever have. That's what they all say about the Crippler. Rick Flair, Arn Anderson, Dean Malenko, Chris Jericho, Chavo Guererro, Edge, Punk, everybody.

Good family man, too. Always showing off pictures of his kid. Always calling home after matches.

46

Shit, Rog says. Probably WWF just messin' with people's heads again. These meatheads thinkin' it's the real fuckin deal, whackin' off to it. Rog making like he's jerking off the handle of his knife all over the omelet bar.

WWE, I say. World Wildlife Fund sued them for name infringement.

Uncle Rog, he's rereading lines from the story over and over and shaking his head. Bullllllll... shit...he's telling me.

Bullllll... shit. he's saying again.

Scripted, I mumble. Not fake.

There's a fan right beside the flattop, big vent right above. I could probably tell Rog I wanna take that carving knife, turn it sideways, and jam it up his candy ass. Even if he was listening, which he ain't.

You smell what the Rock is cooking? I mutter it into the vent above my head. Bull shit, Rog says. Predetermined, I say. A *work*.

45

Raw originally being scripted to have the whole roster paying final respects to Mr. McMahon all night. Saying what a good boss he'd been. Really tearing up about the tragic accident from the week before, saying if they'd only known how real things could get. How everything was gonna turn out.

Mr. McMahon, who'd only the week before been back feuding with his arch-nemesis again, the Rattle Snake

A Good Ram Is Hard to Find

Stone Cold Steve Austin, when Stone Cold'd finally taken his feud a bit over the edge. Blammo! Blows up Mr. McMahon's limo in the parking garage on live TV to end the episode.

Which, all this leading up to this week's big televised funeral, where old Stone Cold at some point would come out and read a little bible verse of his own. Call it Austin 3:16.

Proceed to desecrate all the flowers, that shiny coffin. Maybe shower Mr. McMahon's shiny bronzed corpse with a couple shook up Steveweisers. Shake his head in Mr. McMahon's cold dead face, flip him the double birdies. Call him names. Say What? about thirty times and wait for him to say something back. Be real disrespectful about it.

Which'd be when Mr. McMahon would've had enough. Come back to life Undertaker-style. Reach up out of the coffin and grab Stone Cold by the throat. Maybe even pull him down in that coffin with him—trapdoor or something. Real creepy.

But also, world wrestling entertainment at its finest.

Instead, Mr. McMahon has to drop the whole thing, come out and explain the unfortunate irony. Talk about what a loss it is for the wrestling world. Say what a consummate professional the Crippler has always been.

Send his condolences to the family, really emphasize that part, the condolences to the family. The family. And what a great family man Chris always was. Call him by his first name. His Christian name.

Bull fucking shit, Rog says, he's shouting, spitting, pouting. Waving the tip of that knife at the back of my head with little regard for my safety.

44

Rog who's officially Sous Chef Rog to Uncle Wayne's Head-Chef Wayne, officially, though I'm fairly certain neither of them has any actual culinary training. Unless you count all meth that Rog's cooked in his life.

Rog being in charge most of the time when Auntie Carol ain't around. Less for Wayne to worry about, more time for Wayne to sit on his fat ass.

Earn the big bucks, as he calls it. Usually'll pat his belly a little after saying that, then lean back in his swivel chair, put his hands behind his head, and close his eyes for a bit.

Making the big decisions, he says, with a big yawn.

Like hiring Rog and every one of Rog's little meth-head minions. *Reformed* minions, as Wayne is quick to point out.

Never miss a shift, Wayne says. Not Rog, not Sissy, not a one of them minions that Rog's

recommended.

Too much to lose, Wayne says. Probation and all that. Not like some flake college kid, no-shows the first time he gets his hands on a fake ID.

He's always looking straight at me when he says it.

43

Me being an Auntie Carol special.

Auntie Carol's nephew being married to the wrestling coach's daughter, whatever you might call that relationship.

Me needing an actual job to pay for school so I don't have to do this the rest of my life. Or worse. End up sitting on a couch and sucking off the government teat like my ma, my stepdad, my fat-ass stepsister.

Course there's my fake job as a wrestling manager but not the kind of fake wrestling job that gets paid the big bucks or any bucks at all.

Me, just to be part of a team, part of a family. Me, for the love of the sport. The fame and glory.

42

I'm like five-four, maybe a buck fifteen on a good day. Too tall to be a dwarf, too skinny to be a midget. Too scrawny and fragile to be worth a damn in a singlet, let alone sequined tights.

But that doesn't stop me from helping out the team. Wipe the mats, fill the water bottles. That type of thing. The manager, though sometimes the guys'll call me the ball boy when they're trying to get under my skin.

As in: Hey ball boy, fetch me some fresh water.

Or: Coach, can we get that ball boy over here to wipe these mats for once. They stink like piss.

Or: Hey ball boy, you wanna give deez a wipe down too? What's that? Deez nuts?

But I don't let it bother me.

The closest I'll ever come to being a wrestler. The wrestling manager. Even if it's not the Classy Freddie Blassie kind.

41

It'd only taken me about a week of flipping eggs here, I come to find out I'm the only one works in restaurant who ain't never bought drugs from, sold drugs for, and/or a bit of both from Uncle Rog.

Once a day I got big Sissy coming up behind me while I'm grilling up a side of bacon. Sniff my neck a couple times, scrunch up her face. Then sniff some more. My ears, my hair, my face and chest.

I smell bacon, she says. Then to back Rog: You smell bacon, Rog?

Smells like bacon to me, Sissy, he says. Then: Better give that one there a little pat down. That there's an Auntie Carol hire.

To which Sissy starts grabbing and stroking the insides of my ankles, my thighs, the outsides of my hips, ribs, armpits. Sticks her finger in and around my mouth like she's checking for cavities.

Finishes it all up by reaching up between my legs, getting a good handful, goosing it a couple times, then sliding on back up through the bony craters of my ass cheeks.

Can't be too careful, Sissy tells Rog when she's done with me. All the places they be stashing wires these days. Finishes it all off with good hard pat on the rump.

This is my life. What I get for wanting to make something with my life. Earn my own way. For not wanting to be a leach on society like everybody else I grew up with.

40

I'm tossing a couple juicy sausage links on the flat top. Hundred percent pork. Fatty as hell. Listening to the grease sizzle a little as it spills out. Going to town chopping them up with the side of my spatula.

You telling me these jokers go on national teevee, kiss the man's ass for three hours after he's killed his wife and kid?

What kind a man? Rog keeps muttering. He's marching back to ask Uncle Wayne in the office. What kinda man, Chef? he asks Uncle Wayne.

Wife, maybe. Sure I can figure that, but some little kid? Real tough guy. Killin' his goddamn little kid.

Just cut your dick off, motherfucker. Do the world a favor. Bleed to death. Ain't that tough enough for you?

If I didn't already know everything I know about Rog—how much meth he's cooked and sold in his life, how many knee-caps he's smashed, how many lives he's threatened over a few missing pills—I might think he's actually torn up about all this.

39

For the record, Uncle Rog is not my uncle, the same way Uncle Wayne is not my uncle, the same way Auntie

Carol ain't my auntie, old senile Grandma up at the host station ain't my grandma. Same way big Sissy out waiting tables sure as shit ain't my big sister.

But like it says out there on the sign: *Andersons Family Restaurant: Real Good Food, Real Good Family Atmosphere.*

And as Uncle Wayne puts it, since we're never gonna be confused with real good food, then we're obliged to put on a convincing show for the second part.

Keep that woman from chewing the rest of my ass off, Wayne says.

Just look at my sad, sad ass, Jermy, he says and pulls up the back of his chef coat. There ain't no more ass for that woman to chew off.

Auntie Carol being *that woman*, not being an Anderson herself, but being Wayne's wife—actual wife—and as Rog puts it, the one wearing the big-boy pants in the relationship. The balls of steel, the designated swinging dick.

In charge of the whole thing and making a point to pop her head in the restaurant a couple two three times a day just to make sure we're maintaining the façade.

Far as I know, there ain't one actual Anderson among us.

38

Auntie Carol comes back, pokes her head in to remind me, the way she does every day.

Don't forget, Jeremy. She's tapping her watch. Twelve o'clock sharp, she says. Makes that squinty-eyed smile at me, all cheeks, no teeth.

Egg whites only of course, she says. Eight-six onions and peppers. Sub turkey sausage.

Calls back over her shoulder: You know how your Auntie Carol's watching her cholesterol.

Then heads out to kiss a little customer ass on her way back down to the basement. Manager's office, aka the torture dungeon.

We don't have turkey sausage. We've never had turkey sausage so long as I've been here. But that's never stopped her from asking for it, so it's never stopped me from pretending to give it to her.

Yes ma'am, I say after she's left.

Anything you say, ma'am, I say. Grab my junk good and hard, with a little pelvic thrust thrown in there for good measure.

37

Sometimes Coach'll let me tussle a little at practice, maybe roll around with the flyweights, have me try to get out from under their holds and pins.

You could say that's my specialty, I guess. Squirming.

My patented finishing move—if I were an actual rassler—how to wiggle my way out from under the body slams of even the biggest strongest fattest sweatiest of heels.

Just call me the Worm.

If I were an actual midget, I think I could for sure make it as a wrestler, at least as a midget who'd interfere with all the matches. Get people to chase me.

And then run away. Never let anybody catch me. Get them all counted out while my normal-sized wrestler buddy would just stand in the ring and yell, Run Wormy run!

If only I were a little shorter, fatter.

<u>36</u>

Uncle Wayne, days he's feeling extra family-like, he'll sneak up from behind me while I'm at the grill. Throw different submission holds on me. Full Nelsons, Cobra Clutches, sometimes just your good old fashioned sleeper hold.

I'll teach you to rassle, he'll tell me. Pick me up and shake me around like a rag doll. You ready to tap, boy? he'll ask. A moment later: You ready for night-night?

The other day he goes and drops his wallet in front of his office door. Jermy, he tells me. Be a pal and get that for old Uncle Wayne? he says. He's rubbing his back, making like he's big Sissy and seven months pregnant.

Back's killing me, he says.

Only, when I go to bend over and pick it up for him, he's straddling the back of my neck with them sweaty-ass thighs of his. Hoisting me up backwards, hanging me upside down for a pile-driver.

And he may've protected my head like a seasoned pro when he kicked his legs out and flopped back on the tile floor, but still.

Rog over there reading the newspaper same as usual and doing nothing but egging him on. Yah, Chef, he says. Teach that boy some manners.

Nobody ever seems to worry too much if my eggs might be burning or if Wayne really might be cutting off my windpipe, or in danger of dropping me by mistake, maybe breaking my neck the way Owen Hart once broke Stone Cold's neck. Put him on the shelf for a hole year. Almost ended his career for good.

You know what happens to guys who break other guys' necks by for-real pile driving them too hard by accident? They end up dying a couple years later when nobody checks to see if the harness is secure before they try to repel down to the ring from the top of the arena.

Nobody seems to think Wayne's various finishing maneuvers are abusive or inappropriate for a family restaurant.

35

Me and my fat-ass stepsister, we used to wrestle a little bit back when we were kids.

What'd usually happen, me and Dee-Ann, we'd have the front of the house to ourselves, under the condition that we were not under any circumstances to bother my ma while she's back in her bedroom all day watching her stories.

Dee-Ann's old man, first thing in the morning, Dale'd get up off the couch and head out to the bars for the rest of the day to pretend to be looking for a job so the old lady wouldn't kick his lazy ass out once and for all.

Which'd usually end up with Dee-Ann—three years older and at least fifty pounds heavier—coming up from behind me while I'm playing with my rubber wrestling guys, then sitting on the back of my head Yokuzuna-style and bouncing up and down.

You wanna wrestle, eh? she's whispering in between bouncing on my head. You ready to tap out, yet?

C'mon wormy, she's whispering. I thought you were a big tough wrestler guy.

Your wrestling guys are pretty gay by the way, she's whispering.

Your butt is gay, I'm whispering from under her fat-ass butt.

It's all fake you know?

Nuh-uh.

Is too.

Goes on and on about how her dad knows Sergeant Slaughter and he drinks with him all the time and Sergeant Slaughter tells her dad all about how they're all actually friends and they all hang out and get wasted together after all the matches. Talk about how gullible all those stupid little boys are who think it's real and play with their gay wrestling dolls.

Nuh-uh, I say. Is not.

Yeah-huh, she says.

<u>34</u>

Rog's back behind me waving that knife around again. Well, I'm waitin', Jermy. Waitin' for you to explain this wrestling shit to me.

You's the wrestler, ain't you?

I actually stop what I'm doing, turn around, and say it loud and clear as I can: Roids, man, shit. Then: The bigger the muscles, the tinnier the wiener, I say. The fuck should I know? I'm actually facing him when I say it, staring down the tip of that knife.

Shit, I say. Maybe he got jealous. I'm back to mumbling now. Back to flipping my eggs, rolling Auntie Carol's omelet nice and tight like a burrito.

Maybe he caught his old lady checking out his kid's dingaling during bath time, I say. Shit, I just cook the eggs.

That's right, Rog says. I clean forgot. You's one of them leotard fairies, ain't you? One of them—he cups his hands and makes a farting noise—fudge packers.

<u>33</u>

They really wanted to get all the kids around here off the drugs, they'd have a blown-up picture of Rog up there on that meth billboard I pass by every morning on my way to work.

Shit, put him in a commercial, something, anything where they could show all them kids Rog's stringy-ass mullet, where it begins and ends with all that forehead stretching longer and longer in between.

Those six, seven missing teeth, all the ones I've been able to count anyway. That sunken spot in the bottom corner of his jaw where his gums'd started to cave in. The pink scars and purple ravines that cut across his face and forearms. All them jagged blue veins.

His shaking hands whenever he ain't twirling that knife.

Let Rog talk to the kids. Let Rog tell them the type of shit he tells me on a daily basis.

Shoot a close-up of those mix-matched bug-eyes of his—one blue, one brown—as he blinks and blinks and twitches and tells me: You smart-assed me like that a few years back, I'da called up ol Sissy, come pay you a little visit. A house call, you know what I mean.

I'da called up old girl one night and I'da told her I got a little job for ya.

Y'know what she'd say? he asks me. She wouldn't say shit, he says. Wouldn't ask *what for*, wouldn't ask *how hard*, wouldn't ask *how much*.

She'd say, What's the address? Hour later, show up at your back door—midnight or noon, rain or shine, sleet or snow. Introduce you to her two little buddies, her boyfriends, she calls 'em. Taller one named Lucky Louie, shorter one named Stan the Man.

And boy, let me tell you right now, you don't never wanna be on the wrong of end of a house call with Sissy's little boyfriends. These little guys, they ain't cute names for vibrators.

Start the conversation by introducing the back of your head to Louie, and finish the conversation by introducing your knee-caps to Stan the man's flat hard head.

Shoot a documentary of Rog just telling all the druggy kids about his relationship with big Sissy, all the shit she's done for him over the years, everything they done together.

32

Dee-Ann says her dad's friend from work, his uncle was in the army with the Sarge. Says her dad's told her all about it and how the Dale thinks it's really pathetic that kids like me play with all these wrestling dolls when it's not even real and all the wrestlers think I'm a joke.

How Dale says that nobody'd ever pay good money to watch a midget like me get thrown around by grown men anyway.

I don't care, I say, still from up under her butt. I hate Dale anyway.

Wanna call up my dad and ask him right now? He'll tell you.

Uh-uh, I say. I hate Dale, I say.

Fine, have it your way then, she says. Starts shifting her weight from side to side until she lets out the loudest wettest, most vibratingest fart ever. Vibrations reverberating against my ear lobes like they're coming inside my own head. Literal brain farts.

I struggle and struggle to squirm free. Head butt, bite, turn my head this way and that. Make it at least ten or fifteen minutes of Dee-Ann bouncing up and down and grinding my head into the carpet before I give in and start crying.

Mommy!

Goddamn it Jermy, she's yelling from back in her bedroom. How you ever gonna grow up to be a professional wrestler if you start crying every time your sister teases you?

Nobody wants to pay good money to watch a crybaby get thrown around the ring, honey. Suck it up or do something about it, Jermy, but Mommy doesn't want to hear it. Mommy's got stories to watch.

<u>31</u>

It's been raining all morning, God Almighty Himself pissing down on us pretty much since I opened at five. Sounds like we're all stuck inside some old television with no antenna, nothing by white noise.

Occasionally it'll thunder and rattle the dishes a little, make the lights flicker, but other than that, just another beautiful goddamn summer day here at Andersons' Family Restaurant.

None of this changing much about the good life in the Good Food kitchen. Maybe other than a few fewer bitching customers, a couple more complaints than usual from the regulars—old biddies all of them—wouldn't miss a day rain, sleet, or snow to bitch about my cooking. Tell me my eggs is too runny, my toast ain't burnt enough, my bacon's too limp.

Which is real frickin' hilarious, let me tell you. Don't matter how many times I have to hear Sissy come back and tell me.

One time I just went ahead and stuck a handful of uncooked strips down my pants and flapped them around for Sissy and everyone else to see.

How's my bacon now? I keep asking Sissy. It get hard yet?

Right up until Auntie Carol has to poke her sourpuss back there. Squint and squint through them old lady glasses 'til finally she realizes what's sticking out my fly.

You take that bacon out of your pants right now, mister. This is a family restaurant. I... I... I have half a mind to call your coach up right now and ask him how he might feel about your shenanigans.

Other than that it's the same old windowless dungeon, all these dingy-yellow halogens buzzing like bug-zappers.

Maybe the only other thing's changed, radio reception sucks a little worse than usual, which is why I got my mixtape in. Listening to a little Slim Shady til Carol comes back and tells me it ain't family friendly.

<u>30</u>

Rog says to me, he says, Shit, boy. You wanna know tough? My old daddy, he says, he used to wrestle bears.

For money, he says.

Mucho dinero. He's rubbing his thumb and forefingers together with one hand, showing me the money, waving that blade around in my face with his other.

Really, I say, What'd all them bears pay with?

Rog up in my ear, waving that blade up and down as if he's sizing me up for a suit, maybe a coffin.

Wasn't much bigger than you, my daddy.

Now imagine one of them big mama bears around these parts, he says, hoo-boy.

Boy, you think you seen big Sissy pissed off, shit, you don't want to see no big mama bear after they done took her cubs away and chained her up in the middle of the trailer park.

What I'm imagining is a pregnant Sissy with a spiked dog collar around her neck, chained to the basement of that meth shack Rog still lives in out in the boonies. Where Wayne's made me go pick him up from more than a few times. Rog having his license revoked and all.

Sissy playing the dancing bear, Uncle Rog there with his whip and chains trying to tame that awful beast.

29

Back before Dee-Ann's old man'd took off for good, left Dee-Ann behind along with me and Ma, he did take us to see Sergeant Slaughter one time.

It was this flag match, what they called it. There's Sarge marching to the ring with old red white and blue waving from side to side. Playing this song that's supposed to be vaguely patriotic, but not the national anthem or even

Proud to be An American. Aren't any words to it even. Just some uppity drums and horns playing.

Then there's the Iron Sheik, who's already made his way to the ring. What sounded like bag pipes.

Has what I'm guessing to be the Iranian national flag.

First thing, before old Sarge gets out there, Sheik grabs the microphone. Iran number one, he says, waves his flag. Then says: USA—spits on the mat, stomps it in.

Whole crowd goes wild. Dee-Ann's dad even gets up and gives him the thumbs down. Calls him a dirty A-rab. Tells Sheik to go back where he belongs.

Then old Sarge gets up there, makes a big deal out of putting his flag up on the side of the ring and saluting it. Then turns to face Iron Sheik, points back at the American flag, and shouts, Nobody spits on these hallowed grounds and gets away with it, maggot.

And that's how it starts.

28

I check the window, see about five plates ready to go out. Check the time on the tickets. Minimum fifteen minutes.

Ring that order bell three times as loud as I can make it sing. Order up, Sissy! It's been fifteen minutes, Sissy.

Ring it a couple more times just for good measure. Come get your food, Sissy, before it gets cold, and I have to remake it for all them ol' biddies because you're too slow and fat and lazy. Mumble that last part up into the air vent for nobody but me to hear.

Still, when I look back Rog is making eyes at me. Says: You ain't never heard the one about sleeping dogs, boy? How about sleeping bears—big pissed off pregnant snoring bears?

When I look back over to the office, I see Wayne leaning back in his swivel chair, staring at the ceiling.

One of these days, I mutter to myself, head over to check out the latest ticket.

<u>27</u>

Trick is, Rog says, first off, don't be dumb enough to get caught up in a no bearhugging match with no pissed off mama bear.

Stick and move, he says. Puts the knife between his teeth and shows me like some old-time boxer. His fists way out in front of his body. Float like a butterfly, he says, sting like a bee. All that Mohamed Ali shit.

Shit you not, boy, he says. Seen it with my own two eyes. Says this while taking the knife out of his mouth, grabbing the handle, making a devil sign with his pinky and pointer, and pointing that devil sign at his eyes and then over at mine.

Point is, he says, my daddy he ain't never wear no fruity little leotard to wrestle no bear. My daddy'd come straight home from the factory in his coveralls. Strip down to his civvies. Even things out. Give that mama bear something to tear into in between getting slapped around by a guy half her size and only his fists to make conversation with.

Whatchu think about all that, boy? Huh? Still think this rasslin' makes you a big tough guy? Get all hopped up on them roids, shrink your wiener, then take it out on your wife and kids?

Bullllll shit! Rasslin.

I ain't actually a wrestler, I shout a minute later, after he's headed back to smoke with Sissy.

You hear me? Just a goddamned manager. That's all, I say.

I get the water, do the laundry, wipe the mats. Can't anybody understand that? It ain't the WWE, I shout. It ain't like I'm some Mouth of the South or Mr. Fuji. I sure as hell ain't no Bobby the Brain.

26

It's not long until Auntie Carol hears me bumping some Real Slim Shady. Pops her head back in: Just what is it you think you are listening to now, mister?

I cock my head and squint as if to try to figure out what's playing. After a bit, I shrug my shoulders and go back mumbling, *Will the real Slim Shady please stand up, please stand up?*

Auntie Carol takes a couple steps closer, cups her hands around her mouth. Shouts that she's telling me for the last time. This is a family restaurant, young man. Shouts that we do not listen to that gangster rap here at our family restaurant.

Says it all slow and marbley in her mouth: gang...ster. Like we're some bootlegging outfit for Capone.

Look hee-ah, see... I say out of the side of my mouth as I walk over to turn off my tape. *I ain't taking no orders from some dame, y'hee-ah?*

Shake my fist in the air like I seen in this old timey movie once. *Y'hee-ah?*

25

Just to prove that her dad wasn't no two-faced liar on top of everything else he was and wasn't, Dee-Ann makes him drive us around all night after the match til we finally track down the hotel bar where old Sarge and his buddies are tying one on at.

But Dale, I keep saying, I didn't even bring my Sergeant Slaughter doll. But Dale...

You don't need no damn doll to get an autograph, son, he mutters. He's scrounging around the bar for a couple of cocktail napkins, then an itty-bitty pencil that somebody's left sitting by the dartboard.

It's a goddamned aut-o-graph, boy, he says. All's he gotta do is sign something.

Dee-Ann's shoving me over toward them one bulldozer step at a time. Go on, worm, Dee-Ann's telling me. We don't got all frickin' night.

Over Sarge's shoulder, I recognize Iron Sheik, right away. Then Wahoo McDaniel next to him. Both hunched over half-full pitchers of beer and half-eaten pizzas.

A Good Ram Is Hard to Find

Mr. Slaughter, Dale finally says stepping out from behind me. Sir, he says and gives this real awkward two-fingered salute more like the boy scouts than the Marines.

It's just my wife's kid here, he says, and grabs me by the shoulder, pulls me over next to him. Well, you know.

Everybody's eyes on me now as I look up and look away, hug the napkins and pencil to my chest as tight as I can.

Go on, boy, Dale says and wrenches at my arm again. Ask them man.

The Sarge's all chin and moustache, just like I've seen on TV. But besides that almost unrecognizable without his signature drill instructor hat and aviators.

He sighs a big sigh, then turns almost in slow motion to get a good up and down of me first, then Dale, who's suddenly taking an active interest of the game on the TV back in the corner of the bar behind us.

Mr. Slaughter, I say, hold out my handful of napkins and pencil as far as I can reach. Would you please sign these? I forgot to bring my Sargent Slaughter wrestler doll.

24

Where's Sissy? Auntie Carol wants to know, she's got that sourpuss all puckered up under those glasses of hers.

She's right here, Auntie, I mutter and grab my crotch.

I got my back to her, I'm trying to tune in some CCR or Skynyrd, maybe even some Johnny or Willy or Waylon if nothing else. All two and a half stations we get around here. Anything that won't make me want to stick my head in the deep fryer before noon.

Where's she at?

Where the hell's she ever, I'm muttering. Smoking, sleeping, fucking in dry storage again. Take your pick, lady. Mumble it extra quietly.

Would you turn that crap off for a second? I can't hear a word you're saying. Smoking! I finally shout. She's out smoking in rain. With Uncle Rog.

Jeremy Schmidt, she says. Only person here knows actual name. Be serious, she says. You know well as I do Sissy's about to have that baby.

Cancer baby, I mutter. Spawn of Satan.

Just tell her I'm looking for her, she says. I got papers for her to sign before she goes on leave.

Paid vacation, that's what Sissy calls it. Only way I'm ever gonna get time away from all you freaks and losers, she says.

Says it's Devon's from the garage down the street. Says she been waiting her whole life to have her a big beautiful black baby.

Yah sure, Uncle Wayne says. Devon's. Winks at Rog when he says it.

Eventually I turn the radio back up, blast some Dirty White Boy. I been in trouble since I don't know when, they're singing through the radio fuzz.

I'm in trouble now... I'm singing right along with them. *And I know somehow I'll find trouble again...* My own kind of radio fuzz. *Cause I'm a dirty white boy...*

23

Old Sarge, he takes one last sip of beer shoots another look back at Iron Sheik and Wahoo McDaniel, neither of them looking up from their pizza and pitchers.

Ah Christ, he says, and snatches the napkins out of my hand. Plops the napkin down on an empty spot of the pizza tin in front of him.

Well, who do I make it out to, soldier?

Dee-Ann blurts it out before I can open my mouth: *Worm!* She shouts it and then explodes with giggles. *His name's Jermy the Worm.*

Dale lets out a little titter of his own, before giving Dee-Ann a smack upside the head.

I hear either Sheik or Wahoo let out a big *Ha!* with a mouthful of pizza, then start coughing.

To Jermy the Worm, the Sarge reads out loud as he scribbles unsteadily on the tiny napkin, the wobbly pizza tin. Pencil like a toothpick in that sweaty paw of his.

He takes a long look at it, squints his eyes trying to read his own writing. Looks back at back at Sheik and Wahoo, then back down at me.

Well shit, he says, big smile stretching out across that chin of his. Almost forgot to sign my name, he says.

Except instead of signing his name, he goes and wipes his mouth with it. Smears the pencil scratches over with pizza sauce and slobber.

Looks at it again, squints. Ah Christ, he says, now where are my manners?

22

I'm glancing back at the last plate of eggs been sitting in the window for close to ten minutes now, I'm dinging the bell again and hollering bloody hell for Sissy.

Oh Sissy, I'm yelling in between dings. Your food's getting cold.

Outside it sounds like the rain is coming down even harder. Wherever it is Rog and Sissy have holed up to get a heater and stay dry.

Eventually Wayne wakes up from making all his big decisions, gets up off his ass and waddles over to the kitchen.

Now where the hell Rog and Sissy run off to again?

21

Sheik and Wahoo are doubled over with giggles behind Sarge's broad shoulders, making googly eyes at each other like teenaged girls. Dale and Dee-Ann both tittering quietly behind me.

Sarge craning his head back now, his face all scrunched up as if he's about to sneeze. Except instead of sneezing, he only sniffs and snorts, eventually sucks up pretty much all the snot he can muster, probably all the snot any of us can muster aside from maybe Dee-Ann.

Sarge now holding up the tiny napkin to his nose and letting loose with the biggest wettest, loudest of nose-blows ever known to man. We're talking a nose-blow the sound a vacuum makes when you stick your lips down the hose and see who can suck harder.

One of them nose-blows where you need another whole Kleenex just to wipe up all the overflow snot from the first Kleenex, which is just what he uses the other napkins for that I've handed him.

I can hear Dale cough out the last of his giggles, then edge closer to me. Now you just hold on a second there, mister, he starts to say.

But before Dale can step around me or come up with anything else to say, the Sarge is balling up all the napkins together, wiping excess snot and pizza sauce off his hand and handing it all back to me, my hands out like I'm taking communion or something.

God bless you soldier, he's saying, that big booming baritone of his. He's saluting me a full-on Marine salute, though not actually standing up off his stool or looking in my direction.

Now get the hell outta here why don'tcha. Let old Sarge and his comrades drink in peace.

20

Eventually, Grandma comes back and starts eating bacon off the window. Goes at it like an ally cat eating bubble gum off the bottom of a Dumpster.

This food's cold, she says and works at a couple more bites. You're old, I mumble and turn back to the grill.

You're gonna have to remake this, she says.

You're gonna die soon, I say.

She's moved on to the hash browns. This food's too cold, Jermy.

Like your lifeless corpse.

Where's Sissy?

When I turn back, the old lady's pulling a fork out of her pocket. I yell for Sissy over my shoulder.

Grandma yells her name too: Sissy! Like somebody's just dropped a cement block on that cat's hind legs.

I ring the bell about eight more times. Grandma's looking for you, Sissy! I yell over my shoulder. Auntie's looking for you too, Sissy! I yell. Food's cold Sissy. Nobody wants it now, Sis—

19

When the big one hits, it rattles everything, knocks out the lights completely. Everything goes quiet for a moment, except for the old biddies out in the restaurant, sighing and moaning, me wishing that I couldn't imagine what their sex sounds sounded like.

Ooooh... I say. Scary.

You ever stop talking, boy? It's Wayne come back out from the office, up off his fat ass for the probably second time all morning.

But it's the rapture, Wayne, I say. Ooooh...

Jermy, Wayne says, that's enough.

But it's the rapture, Wayne, I say again when the lights still haven't come back on. It's the reckoning, I say.

Start banging my spatula on the grill, banging the pots and pans hanging next to it.

Jermy shut your ass, Wayne says. I can hear him stumbling his way over to try and put a headlock on me.

He's coming, Wayne, I start shouting, He's coming, He's coming to take us away!

First Mr. McMahon, then the Crippler, now us. We have to pay, Wayne. Pay for the sins of Rog and Sissy. The birth of their spawn.

18

What it was, me and Dee-Ann'd both gotten a bit older. A couple more years under our belts, a few more pounds for one of us, about fifty or sixty more pounds for the other.

And maybe that was it. Maybe Dee-Ann'd simply lost her youthful vigor, as they say. Maybe she'd simply grown tired of pinning me and sitting on my head and pulling my arms back and sometimes my legs til it seemed every bone in my spine might pop out one at a time. Make those little ping- ping-ping noises the way cartoons make it sound with a rope gets stretched to its breaking point.

Whatever reason, she can't muster up much enthusiasm to hold her submissions anymore. Doesn't even bother waiting for me to give up squirming and call for Mommy.

Ah Christ, she says one day. Rolls off me completely. You pathetic little worm. All this gay wrestling you watch and you still can't even put up half a fight worth my time.

I'm sitting up and rubbing carpet burns off my cheeks and forehead.

Bet you couldn't even pin me if I laid there and gave you a two-count head start. Yeah-huh, could too, I say.

How much you wanna bet? Million dollars.

You ain't even got no ten cents.

Yeah-huh, I say. I got almost five whole dollars saved up from cleaning out the couch cushions. Show me, she says.

You don't have to be an expert on wrestling to know a setup when you see it coming.

17

Don't you be making fun of no rapture, boy. First it's Rog's voice coming from around the corner. Then it's Sissy from a bit further down the back hallway: What's that spaz saying now?

The lights are on by the time I turn to see them making their way back from dry storage, both of them tucking things in, re-adjusting articles of clothing.

Boy's making jokes about the coming apocalypse, Rog says.

That shit ain't funny, freak-boy, Sissy says. She's trying to tie her apron back on way down underneath all that belly, stretching them sausage fingers out far as they'll go. Some of all that bulge being a baby, possibly the spawn of Satan.

This ain't no time to be joking about no end times, she's saying, patting her belly now with both hands, rubbing them around the lumpy circumference of it all, massaging the baby, pointing that bulging volcano of hell right in my direction.

Mess around and God Almighty'll shoot a lightning bolt up your ass, boy, she tells me. Then to her belly: Nuh-uh, not while me and my little Jayshawn standing in the same kitchen as you won't.

You mean Rog Jr.? I mutter. I wander off and ring the bell a couple more times. Order up, Sissy, I say. Food's getting cold, Sissy.

Sissy, Grandma's saying still, again, the sound of that dying cat somebody oughta put out of its misery.

Sissy, this food's too cold now. Old lady's got that fork out, mixing the yolks in with the hash browns and bits of bacon. She's talking with half a mouthful of yellow and gold mush spilling out her rotten teeth.

I told Jeremy he's gonna have to remake this. You can't serve this now, don't you think, Sissy?

16

Dee-Ann having herself a pretty substantial set of boobies on her by then. Not that I was some perv or something. Makes it harder to get leverage is all. Hard to get a good grip on anything.

Plus there's all that greasy face to consider, the zits, the zit cream, all that sweaty neck fat only inches away. Almost worse to deal with than her smothering crotch pins.

But such were the stipulations of our final match.

Me on top for once. Pretty much my whole scrawny body draped across her chest, her lungs going crazy underneath me. My right arm barely holding on to all that thigh of hers as I pull the leg up toward me. Leverage it best I can, considering the weight and strength disparities I'm facing.

One... she says, and takes a deep breath, my body literally rising and falling with each inhale and exhale.

I can see nothing in front of me but those bloodshot whites of her eyeballs, the mounds of reddening flesh twitching ever so slightly atop her cheek bones. That bulging blue vein running from her forehead down to her eyes.

Two... she says, and takes another breath.

15

Problem with you, boy, Rog says. Rolls up the newspaper and taps me on the nose like I'm a puppy that's shit in the house again.

All this rasslin' business be messin' with your head. Giving you this false sense of security. That mouth of yours always runnin' and you ain't got no clue about consequences and repercussions. Real life type shit, let me tell you.

Rog putting down the newspaper and picks back up his knife. Rog shaking that knife at me and telling me about how him and the old lady are going at it one night a few years back. All fucked up, he says, rolls them buggy eyes back in his skull until I can see only the bloodshot whites. Starts like he's humping the oven door.

How he's just managed to pass out for the first time in like a week. How she's just kept on going at it by herself. How pretty soon after he's out cold she starts mixing in the ludes. Gets her hands on a filet knife.

I can smell it on you, she keeps telling him, he keeps telling me. Keeps smelling the crotch of my pepper pants and making stink faces as demonstration.

Smell that lying cheating cunt Sissy on you, he tells me, knife inches away from my junk, finger pointed at my nose. I can't take no more your damned lies, he says, and does a little half-assed Zorro swipe down there.

Baby, he keeps yelling at her, at me. He's scurrying back against the headboard, or in this case the microwave at the end of the line. Cupping my dingaling dear life, he says.

He's acting all this out for me—both parts, himself cupping himself and his old lady swinging that knife around, this bug-eyed look in his/her eyes. Pants on, at this point anyway.

It's yours, he keeps yelling at her, at me. It's you, baby, he pleads with me. It's your own nasty stank-ass cunt, baby. It's all you. Probably ain't washed or douched it in week and a half. God knows how long.

This whole time she ain't stopped reaching and grabbing and lunging for it with one hand, he tells me. Swinging that fuckin filet knife with the other.

14

It's now or never, I think to myself as I lie there atop Dee-Ann's jittery chest. I know what I have to do. You could even say it's predetermined, even if it isn't exactly scripted.

Three! I shout and in one fluid motion, I let her leg slip out from under my forearm, while dropping my elbow—Macho Man style, if not from the top buckle, then at least with the same bony edge to it, right on the money spot, that fragile zipper holding her jeans together for dear life.

All the while I'm posturing up, the recoil of my elbow drop to propel myself forward, my feet driving against the carpet. I can feel her chest, those hot mountainous boobies—desperately trying to erupt underneath me, but not quickly enough.

I have my opening and I'm taking advantage. Her head tilted up just enough, her eyeballs bulging, mouth gaping. I go for it. Those lips, all those crooked teeth. That slimy monster lurking down waiting to be tamed.

I have it locked in. Hard and tight. My body stiff as a board and planked precariously above her with all my weight pressed down through my lips, my probing tongue. Everything around me so very fuzzy and underwater.

13

Rog's got me cornered in the back of the kitchen now, carving knife in one hand, his other grabbing at my junk, my thigh, my butt, my hip, as I cup myself and press back against the cooler. Me not really acting.

And just when I think I got her calmed down, he tells me. I says, Baby give me the knife. And like a real dumbass, I go and reach out for it. Baby, I says, as I let go of myself and put everything out there for her. And just like that, he says. Bam!

Crazy bitch goes all in, he tells me. Lunges at me, at... it.

And sure this ain't my first rodeo, you know? he tells me, taps the side of his head, winks. I manage to block the initial attack.

But see, that ain't never what gets you, boy. Taps his head again. It ain't never the initial thrust, he says, the one you see coming. It's the follow-through, he says. That's the one. Shows me how he blocks her with his forearm, but how the knife keeps going off to the side.

He's pulling his pants down now, standing up like Captain Morgan, one foot pressed up against the side of oven. He's not even hopping or losing his balance, like a regular ballerina. Has that carving knife tucked up in the skin behind his knee. Shows me the inch and a half pink worm running up the inside of his thigh.

What the hell you go and do that for? he's yelling, at her, at me.

Good six inches deep, he says and pats his thigh. Go ahead, he tells me. Touch it. Juiciest part of the inner thigh. The good stuff.

Has his chili-pepper pants all the way down to his ankles now, like he wants me to get down on my knees and ask him to cough.

Go ahead, he tells me again and slaps himself. Touch it.

Grabs me by the hand and pulls my fingers to it. Both warm and scaly at the same time.

Feel that, boy? That there's true love. Somethin' you wouldn't know nothin' about, now would ya?

All the drugs in the world, he says and pulls back out the knife, pulls up his pants. And did I go and kill the crazy bitch?

Did I kill the bitch, he says again as he turns to walk out the kitchen. Fuckin' rasslin', man.

12

It takes me a second to realize the words aren't coming from where I've pinned Dee-Ann's lips, tongue, throat. How long Dale's been standing just inside the doorway, door swung wide open behind him.

What... the... hell...?

These being the last words I can remember Dale ever saying to me before he took off and left my ma to raise me and Dee-Ann both. I can't tell you what he said next, what I said, where my ma might've been to put in her own two cents.

I remember only Dee-Ann bucking me off and sitting upright. Dee-Ann wiping my slobber off her lips and staring down at her hand, how she couldn't take her eyes off that last bit of saliva coating the inside of her thumb.

Daddy! I remember her saying eventually. Almost crying as she says it.

Daddy! I can remember her saying again. A pitch I've never heard her hit before or ever again.

Please, I can remember her saying, the swiftness of her movements as she seemed to spring to her feet.

Daddy, I remember her saying over and over, it's not what you think, it's not what you think.

11

Come noon and the rain has finally let up. Not that there's a lot of sunshine and rainbows peeking through back in the Good Food kitchen.

It's scary quiet. Pretty much all the old biddies gone home for the day. Lunch crowd just starting to filter in. Uncle Wayne back in the office sitting on his ass, Rog and Sissy nowhere to be found. The usual.

Grandma's back telling me that Auntie Carol told her that she's waiting on her omelet still. She's tapping on her watch and telling me, She's a very busy woman, you know? She doesn't have time for this.

Who's a very busy woman? I say.

You know... she says. Carol.

She say that or you say that? I say. I turn around, point my spatula at her accusingly.

Very busy, she says, then clicks her tongue and shakes her head at me. She's running her wrinkly fingers up and down the window shelf longingly. After a couple passes, she picks up a few crumbs of something on the tip of her finger, examines it, then sticks out that little bloodless tongue of hers. Licks.

How many times I've seen that goddamned little blue tongue since I been working here. Enough to have the nightmares, let me tell you.

Jesus, Grandma, I say. Stop that. Take the spatula and smack the window about two inches away from her. No, I say. Bad Grandma. Get.

<u>10</u>

To make things clear: I may enjoy a good old fashioned fake wrestling match from time to time, bunch of oiled up guys running around in tight-tights and sometimes having to pick each other up with one hand over each other's bulging crotches.

I may even be the guy in charge of walking into a locker room full of naked runty college kids playing grab ass after every practice. The privilege this earns me? To gather up all the dirty, sweaty jock straps and singlets that it's then my job to wash and fold and get back to them by the next day.

I may never've had no girlfriend. I may never've even gotten laid, but this all doesn't mean I'm a fudge packer or some sister fucker. Doesn't mean that there aren't perfectly good reasons. Doesn't mean that if you'd've grown up the way I did and seen half the shit I've seen, heard, felt, and been felt by. Doesn't mean you wouldn't understand perfectly where I'm coming from. That you wouldn't be just as messed up about love and lust and the opposite sex as I am.

9

Well? Grandma's asking me, tapping her watch the same way Auntie Carol does.

Well, what?

Did you make it, yet? she asks. What?

Carol's omelet.

About eight times now.

Where is it then?

Right there.

Where?

Up my ass, Grandma. Where?

Go away.

Don't forget, she calls back before finally wandering back to front of the restaurant. Only egg whites, she says. Turkey sausage, she says.

I'll get right on that, Grandma, I say. Grab my crotch again for nobody in particular.

8

There's this one time, I'm just watching some wrestling tapes in living room, minding my own business, choreographing all the moves with my wrestling dolls.

At the same time, I'm having to overhear Dee-Ann go on and on with her newest twenty-something potential future baby-daddy.

What are you wearing, she's saying, this giggly voice I've never heard before.

She's tucked up in the breakfast nook. Only phone we've got, not even cordless, and pretty soon it gets so I can't barely concentrate on the match at hand.

No you...
No you first... No... Well... Okay... Nothing...
Like totally...
Yah, silly. Totally totally.
No, totally...
Well come over here then... I'll prove it to you.
Ah... skip work.
I'll make it worth your while... Don't you love me...?
Don't you want me...?
Ah fuck this, she says at one point.
Hold on a second, babe. I gotta take care of a little pest.

7

Oh Sissy, I yell over my shoulder. I'm making Auntie Carol's omelet again. You better not forget about it this time.

Mumble under my breath: Come back there and shove it up your fat ass, maybe you'll remember then.

One of these days, Wayne calls out from back in the office. I'm telling you, you don't watch out, one of these days one of these here women gonna back there and sit on you, use you like a cheap tampon.

I got my Slim Shady back on now. *Hi... My name is... My name is...*

You hear, me, Jermy?

Chicka-chicka... I'm singing while I separate egg whites for another omelet for Auntie.

One of these days, Jermy?

One of these days, Jermy, I mutter to myself in my Wayne voice. Spread out the whipped egg whites on the flat top, scoop up a spatula-full of greasy fatty regular pork sausage, drop it on top.

Jermy...?

Shake my bony little finger at myself. *One of these women here gonna come sit on your face... Then what'll you have to say for yourself?*

6

My little Iron Sheik doll's got Sarge locked in the camel clutch. Don't you want me, baby? little Sheik's saying.

He's sitting down hard on the Sarge's rubber back, wrenching his rubber head back til it looks like he might rip it clean off.

Don't you love me? Sheik's saying.

Shut up, gaywad, Sarge's saying. Shaking his fists so the ref knows he's not about to tap out. Trying to channel the crowd chanting: *U-S-A... U-S-A...*

I can feel the floorboards shake with each closing step, but I don't bother to look back.

What's she gonna do to me she hasn't done before? I can remember thinking. Remember thinking: This ain't my first rodeo.

When I feel her hands cupping my cheeks first and not her thighs, I know immediately something's wrong.

Maybe this is why I've left my mouth gaping wide open for a surprise attack. It's her stubby nose that I feel next as it bops my own nose, then keeps going. For a second I'm confused. Why's she sticking her nose down my throat, why's it so wet, so slimy? How's she wiggling around and around it like that?

Everything being so dark and wet and confusing, all the light in the room suddenly eclipsed by so much hot flesh pressed up against my face.

Everything so underwater, as if I can hear that slurping and gurgling from inside my own head. As if our bodies have morphed into one.

This monstrous, wet nose worming its way down my through and nearly drowning me. Looking for

what, I don't know.

A moment later it's over, she's licking her lips and wiping her face on the inside of her arm. She's reaching down to hammer-fist me in the nuts.

Whispering in my ear: *Gaywad*. Then turning and waddling back to the breakfast nook, back to the phone.

But baby... she's back to whining.

But baby, I'm so hot right now...

<u>5</u>

I wait about ten minutes, ring the bell a good twenty times before I grab the plate myself and go looking for Sissy.

Oh Sissy... where are you...?

Come out, come out wherever you are...

I know exactly where she is of course. Where both of them are and what they're doing. Sissy, you in there? I yell loud as I can and knock three times on the door to dry storage. Housekeeping, I say in this high-pitched voice.

Go away, freak, I hear her yell.

I knock again. But Auntie Carol needs her fatty omelet, I say.

Knock couple more times. I'm carrying the plate up above my right shoulder pressed up high on my fingertips. Delivering a little room service.

Well, go give it to her then, she shouts.

Knock, knock, I say. Finally start to crack open the door slowly and softly as I can. Without looking in, I reach in the half-opened door hold the plate out. Room service, I say.

Right as I say it, the door flies all the way open, revealing Sissy, more red-faced and out of breath than usual.

What is your problem, boy?

She's hitching up her pants underneath her belly, pulling her shirt down where her apron should be hiding everything. I can't help but see those stretch marks and varicose veins burned into my eyeballs for all eternity.

Back in the shadows I can just make out the outline of Rog draped over a crate of flour bags. His head propped up against the shelf where we keep the potatoes. He's got one hand resting on his bare chest, chef coat completely unbuttoned. With the other he's pinching a doobie, lips puckered up at me, blowing smoke rings.

Go away, freak-boy, Sissy says. Takes my hand with the omelet and serves it back to me. Shoves me back out into the hallway.

Closed for lunch, she says. Slams the door in my face.

<u>4</u>

I wait 'til I hear Sissy take a few steps back, then knock again. Oh Sissy, I say. Auntie Carol needs you to bring her her omelet. Needs you to sign some papers for her before you go on vacation, I say.

By this time, I'm gently slipping the door open just enough to reach in with the omelet again. She's a very busy woman, I'm saying.

Without looking, I'm gently setting the plate down just inside the door quickly and quietly as I can.

I'm closing the door that way too.

Probably saying the next thing a bit louder than I need to. A little excited, a little caught up in the heat of the moment.

I shout over my shoulder, I say, Auntie Carol says she don't want you to sue the restaurant when your cancer baby comes out all deformed and retarded.

<u>3</u>

I'm walking briskly now. I'm listening as the door swings open. Those footsteps, those thundering footsteps, coming behind me.

What'd you say, freak? Sissy's booming voice echoing down the halls from behind me.

I'm at a trot now back to the kitchen, my feet slipping and sliding on the greasy tile floor as I turn the corner. As I feel my feet go out from under me, as I slip down, then immediately pop back up. All my wrestling training coming back to me.

Whoa, whoa, whoa, what's the big emergency? Uncle Wayne's saying from out of the office. Slow down before you hurt yourself, he's telling me.

You better run, boy! Sissy is yelling from behind, breathing heavy.

I make for the double-doors out to the restaurant, but then there's Grandma and Auntie Carol both standing there cross-armed and scrunching up their pruny faces at me.

Just what in tarnation is going on here? Auntie Carol is saying.

Jermy! Grandma is yelling. Sissy! Grandma is yelling. Carol here is waiting for her omelet.

I make for the back corner of the kitchen, I make for the flat top, I make for the rack of pots and pans behind it. I'm not sure what my move is, but I'm looking for as many possible shields as I can.

<u>2</u>

It's thundering again, everything shaking, but no rain coming down. The radio back on the fritz. This might very well be the end times. The four horsemen coming for me, but not the ones wearing wrestling tights.

The lights in the kitchen don't go off, don't flicker, but I do close my eyes for a moment. Imagine this is all just another work dream. One of those dreams where I'm twelve tickets deep and no one else there to help me but Grandma licking everything I put in the window.

Looking for something? Sissy's voice only inches away now. The stench of weed and that bottle of Febreeze Rog keeps back there for just such occasions.

Whoa, whoa, whoa, Wayne is saying from somewhere over my shoulder. Let's all just cool our jets a bit here, eh?

You done pissed off the wrong mama bear now, boy. It's Rog from a bit farther back. That mouth of yours, I done told you, he's saying, as he makes his way towards the kitchen.

Will someone please tell me what is going on here? Auntie Carol is saying.

What I feel first is that big sweaty mitt of hers palming my face. It's so warm, soft. For a moment I imagine taking a nap in it.

I'm thinking of all those times Dee-Ann'd engulfed me with those thighs of hers, that one time she'd nearly drowned me with that Loch Ness monster of a tongue.

I'm thinking about the Crippler. That poor little-dicked bastard. What kind of pep talk he must've had to've given himself to be able to throw on his finishing maneuver, what he must've been telling his wife and kid right up to the point they could no longer tap out. The moments after.

I'm up on my tip-toes and puckering up before I notice that it's Sissy that's doing the puckering for me, using me like a puppet.

Me and Jermy here's just having a little conversation here is all, she's saying. Ain't that right, there, Jermy-wormy?

She turns my head to face Auntie Carol. Tell ol' Auntie, would'ya Jermy, she says, tell her we's just having a little talk. She nods my head for me. I nod my head along with her.

See, Jermy here, he was just telling me how bad he felt about telling all those lies about my baby, weren't you Jermy?

Sissy? I hear Grandma say.

Sissy, I hear Auntie Carol say. Maybe we should all sit down and have a talk. How's that—

What's a matter? Sissy's saying to me. Is pointing my face up at her face, making my eyes meet her eyes, backing me up until I'm leaning against the front of the flat top for balance.

Well, she says, cat got your tongue? Tell these fine folks. Tell everybody all about what you been saying about my baby.

Spawn of Satan, I think, but decide not to say.

She's got my head tilted back over the grill now, I can feel the nobs getting turned up as I bump back against the front panel. My toes barely touching the floor.

Tell ol' Auntie all about these vicious lies you been telling people about me smoking while pregnant.

Tell everyone what a miserable little shit you are.

I can feel the heat from the grill creep up my back, each drop of sweat sizzling as it drips down my spine.

Say somethin' smart now, motherfucker, she's shouting.

I've heard somewhere that you always hear the thunder after the lighting hits. That the rumbling only comes after the actual destruction. That's how you can tell how far it is, the time it takes between seeing it hit and hearing the sound of the thunder roll.

But it's the rumble that I feel first, the shaking of the pots and pans above my head, the plates over by the window.

Everything seeming to vibrate for a moment before the darkness hits. For a second I almost convince myself it's the skin on my back starting to sizzle. Maybe I'm starting to black out from the pain, I wonder. Maybe she's slipped me into a sleeper and I just haven't noticed 'til now how tired I am.

How quickly it hits, that moment of darkness. Just a flicker.

But long enough for me to make move. To kick, or rather to knee. It's not as if I'm aiming for the baby, though it works just the same. Allows me my inch of freedom to squirm and wiggle, to eventually make my momentary escape.

A Good Ram Is Hard to Find

1

By the time I've realized what it is I want to do next, I've already found what I've been looking for all along. Rog's newspaper folded up next the ticket machine, that headline: *Police Suspect Professional Wrestler in Double Murder-Suicide.* That eight-inch carving knife resting on top.

I am not a goddamned wrestler, I'm shouting, pointing the tip of that knife at each one of them. At Sissy bent over in front of the grill. At Wayne at the other end of the kitchen, Rog hiding behind him. At Grandma standing there with her arms crossed in front of the double doors. Auntie Carol right next to her.

I'm just a stupid manager, I'm shouting, I wipe up the mats, do the dirty laundry. Get water, I'm shouting. I'm clutching the knife handle with both hands, waving it like my own personal flag: The United States of Jeremy.

Somehow the lights around the kitchen seem to be growing brighter and brighter with each swipe I take of the stale dingy air around me.

I get in their faces. You hear me? Jeremy, one of them says.

Jeremy, someone else says.

I get in Sissy's face, I get in Wayne's face, I get in Rog's.

Jeremy, they all say. Jeremy. Giving me all my syllables for once.

Do you hear me? I shout. I'm bee-lining it straight for Grandma and Auntie Carol. When they step out of my way, the double-doors out to the restaurant. Heading for the light.

Jer-e-my... they're chanting. Jer-e-my. It's getting louder as I push through the double-doors. I see now that the sun's finally come out. All that light spilling into the front of the restaurant, it's almost blinding.

The screams echoing all throughout the restaurant, deafening.

My national anthem.

Turn it up, I shout as I wave my flag high for all the people to see. Get up, I'm yelling. Put your hands over your hearts. Everybody. Show some respect.

How Much I Want You to Love Me

Look how repulsive I've grown over the years. Yours truly three hundred and fifty pounds of straight trans fats, triglycerides, and stretch marks as far as the eye can see. Or as far south as the frayed threads of my wifebeater will reach down my distended beer gut.

This half-assed mohawk because, let's be honest, I'm overcompensating for being so incredibly fat and a lowly fry cook instead of working the land like my old man—who doesn't have a mohawk, doesn't need a mohawk, he has his hands—those hands, I'll get back to those.

In addition to my thread-bare wifebeater, I've got my boxers with holes in the crotch and so bunched up under insides of my sweaty thighs right now that if you were about to give me a blowie under the desk, you'd think I had on a pair of really saggy man-panties, which is just one of the reasons you wouldn't be under the desk in the first place.

I had a girl put her hand down my pants once to get a feel of things, and that was the last I ever heard from her. She couldn't quite get over the fact that it was all shaved off down there. Something queer about it, she was probably thinking. Both strange and homosexual is what I mean by queer.

Sure, she was a good sport and tried to get things going down there for a while, but she kept bristling at the way the stubble felt against the palm of her hand. That's my pun. Bristle. Anyway, she couldn't stop stopping between strokes to wrinkle her little nose at me and sigh this big sigh as if I were asking her to give me some butt play.

This was back before my wife, back before I was quite such a tubbo, but after the hernias, which were just a couple of the reasons. She was my one and only redhead and I never held that against her, nor the fact that she wasn't shaved or waxed, that goddamned jungle of ginger pubes my fingers had to untangle just to reciprocate. And I did reciprocate, by the way. And with none of this sighing and nose-wrinkling business either.

This is how I get people to like me, if you haven't noticed, this bit about me reciprocating and how the ungrateful bitch never called me back after that.

Or maybe just pity. My whole life. Pity and trying to get people to like me.

Like my father, for one.

And chicks with low self-esteem for another. Some of them being redheaded and unshaven.

In my book, pity and liking somebody are basically the same. But also why I'm so goddamned fat all of sudden.

The Hardees around the corner, like twelve empty SURGE!'s cluttering my desk, my life blood, which sometimes tastes a little too much like crystal meth, which I've never had, but from what I've heard.

I was a fry cook for a couple years. The sous chef from nights, he used to tell me how he'd have to have a couple beers for breakfast every morning just to come down before heading off to work.

He tried to stab me once to make a point about never walking behind another cook who's dicing a tubful of onions.

He probably wasn't really trying. It seems like he was the type of guy who would've gone ahead and stabbed me if he was trying. Not to get into any character assassination or anything. You don't even know him. And he wasn't half bad to work with. A helluva cook.

Which is my little joke, or pun. Or maybe not even. Just me making things all sad and awkward again.

Back to my dad's hands. Ham hocks but with these stubby little sausage fingers. Strongest goddamn fingers you'll ever feel patting you on the back. I never did, but I could imagine. Man could twist out fully embedded wood screws that I couldn't even get with two hands and all my weight on the screwdriver.

You probably don't believe that but it's true. Or it was when I was ten years old. Which is sometimes what I do.

Lies by omission, half-truths.

Take for example: I haven't told you that after fifteen years, my wife wouldn't be caught dead under my desk eyeing up my bunched-up undies.

Or washing and folding them, for that matter.

Once before, way back before we started dating, she asked my buddy Todd what to give me for my birthday. What did he say?

He said *The fuck you think you give him, lady. You give that man a beej. Christ. Hasn't he been through enough?*

That's what my friend called a BJ. He was from West Virginia. This accent like Yosemite Sam doing an impression of Barney Fife. But don't worry. I'm not going to try to capture that shit on paper. It's too good.

Anyway, my father, my mem-whas.

Maybe you've heard of it? I called it *Bend with the Knees and Other Love Advice from My Father*.

Which is hilarious to me because my father has never given love advice to anyone so far as I know. Never even kissed my mom while I was around.

But it ain't like my old man molested me or anything, if that's what you're thinking.

Seems to be what those publisher people thought the implication was, that somewhere in there was a metaphor for my dad giving me the old bad touch when I was a little kid. The subtext is what they kept telling me. Or maybe the title.

Metaphors coming to bite me in the ass again.

Again with the jokes.

Probably the only reason they agreed to publish the damn thing in the first place. Thinking they could've gotten me grilled by Oprah on national television or something.

But then maybe that was the problem: too much subconscious molestation subtext, not enough loud and clear molestation in the text.

My dad didn't molest me, you gotta believe. I would've been more than happy to've used that to sell books if he had.

But he did always used to yell at me for lifting hay bales with my back and instead of my knees. But then I went and showed him. Broke the school record for deadlifting in high school. Then about ten years later went and got me a couple of hernias for my trouble. The ones where they shave you down there and then you gotta go and shave your treasure trail yourself otherwise things look a little funny. The road to nowhere.

Now that's fucking funny.

Sometimes I just kill me.

Get it?

But god's honest truth, I did write a book of my mem-whas a few years ago and they even published the silly little thing.

Local farm boy goes and tries to kill himself six different times and lives to write about it, the feel-good story of the year.

And there I go trying to make you like me again.

Or feel sorry.

No molestation though.

Prescription painkillers, which accounted for four of those times, are the teenaged drama queens when it comes to methods of suicide. The last time, I didn't even have to get my stomach pumped. Everything was coming back up red and purple by the time I'd gotten to the bottom of that bottle of Wild Turkey.

And again with the half-truths.

It was Kahlua actually. Only thing that girl had to drink at the time.

Which is my little joke: because that goofy girl was me.

But don't worry. In the book, I made sure to exaggerate everything and make it seem as if I really might've had it in me to kill myself in a manly fashion, like say with a well-placed lasso hanging from the hay elevator up in the barn. A lot of long lingering gazes at my father's hunting rifles locked up in our basement.

My mom said that it hurt my old man the worst. The book, the blaming—not the not being able to kill myself, nor the attempt thereof.

She said it always embarrassed him when people from around town would ask him about it. *What's it called then, Boss?*

Bend with the Knees and Other Love Advice from My Father?

Sure is a funny title there, eh Boss?

It any good?

You even read it yet?

As if my father would've read some sissy little mem-wha from his only boy who all he ever could do was piss and moan about everything, and now low and behold, he'd gone and found a way to make a living off it.

A Good Ram Is Hard to Find

There was no talk of if my mom or dad had thought that I had any molestation subtext in there or how they interpreted the title of it.

Figuratively, you know?

I'm not a healthy man, you know, but then again that's why I had to write myself a book. A mem-wha.

Except the molestation part, which probably would've made it more successful.

Not that my father has ever said anything to me about it. Never even read a page of it so far as I know, thank God.

But my mother's read it, and she's said more than enough for both of them. And there I go again trying to make you like me.

In case you haven't noticed not much for subtlety, all my mem-wahs on and on about how sad and pitiful I am.

Me and my wife had an abortion once, or more accurately, she had an abortion and I went to work to flip eggs.

She had to walk past eight of those praying protesters and everything. Or she said she had to. Of course, she wasn't my wife yet then. Which is one of the reasons we probably ended up tying the knot after so many years of just plain old no-hassle cohabitating.

You wanna know what that whole scene looked like?

Fuck you, it looked like the type of scene that you'd wanna punch somebody over.

But then probably I was a bit sensitive because I didn't even have the stones to call into work. I mean, she was pretty adamant about not making it a big deal and just wanting to get it done, but seriously, what kind of man doesn't even have the stones to go along with his girl to get his unwanted baby aborted? What kind of man lets his girl go and walk past all those damn Jesus freaks and their fetus signs by herself?

Seriously, I'm asking because I don't know and now I'm afraid I've let this woman down too many times to go ahead and try to kill myself for a seventh time, though I'd be lying if I said I don't have the box cutter and a juicy vein on my wrist all picked out.

But what're you gonna do? We weren't even sure if we were going to make it through the winter that year. Do you know what egg flippers make? Do you know what they get for insurance coverage so their newborn babies don't end up retarded or dying from the polio?

Do you know how high those therapy bills would've been? How much mine cost my parents?

And just so you know, there's more than a good chance my wife probably won't ever be able to have kids now even if she wanted to, which I sure as hell don't, but she's still on the fence, especially in lieu of this all.

It's like that door at the loony bin locked from the outside, I guess. One day you go and try to turn the knob and realize everything in the sterile hallway lighting's been taken away from you and you're a prisoner of your own suicidal mind with no shoelaces or belt to hang yourself with.

Sorry, I've always been real shit for similes.

And puns.

But one of things I did write in my mem-whas was how my dad used to try to make a man out of me by having me reach my little womanly fingers on up the sheep's love canal during lambing season in the dead of winter. Middle of the night. Sub-zero temperatures.

Just go on now, he'd tell me. You gotta get up in there abouts elbow deep. You're looking for a hoof or a head to snag.

Don't worry, son. You'll damn well know it when you get those fingers around. Talk about metaphors.

Maybe this is part of where that subtext came from, I guess.

Which is really just somewhat of an exaggeration. I've never had my pudgy little hands up the love canal of birthing sheep. My old man would've never trusted a lamb's life in these hands.

But he did make me castrate them ram babies sometimes. Grab on to them testes and yank until the lamb quit bleating, til the lamb went soft and slumped over seemingly dead and de-rammed in your lap.

Which is traumatizing enough to write mem-whas about, don't you think?

My mom sure didn't. And she said my dad wouldn't've either if he hadn't've been too embarrassed to read it in the first place.

On the upside, after the abortion, I'll probably never have to worry about some whiney little mama's boy of mine going and writing some mem-wha about me not hugging him enough and telling him how he's the greatest thing since sliced bread even though he can't even be bothered to roll up his sleeves and get his hands a little dirty and sticky up in the love canal during lambing season.

But there I go again.

Trying to make you like me.

By the way, just so you feel like this was all poetic somehow, I want you to know what all I can see out my window right now: a dog shitting next to my mailbox, some dude in short-shorts and a tank top who's not getting out a baggie, not bending over or kneeling down.

I can smell the stink of the stale sugar pasted to my teeth and gums, the teeth I haven't brushed in a couple, two three days. The sour smell of my sweaty balls, how it lingers on my fingernails for hours after twentieth time I've had to stop writing long enough to unstick them from the sides of my thighs.

And sometimes when I just cradle them for a moment or two to comfort myself.

I can hear the spastic tapping of the computer keys as I use my doughy little fingers to type these words.

I can hear a lawnmower going somewhere down the block, probably a rusty one. There may be duct tape I imagine. I think it's Saturday, but it's summer and I haven't checked a calendar or taught a class for a couple months.

What I'm saying is I'm not entirely sure of why anything is anything today.

I can see the sky, the sun, and a bunch of clouds up there scattered all over the place. Some of them are probably Cumulus, some probably Cirrus or Stratus. Or could be none of that's true.

Could be I don't remember jack shit from seventh grade science.

Could be I'm just fucking with you.

Could be I've been making this thing up the whole time and calling it true.

Could be I've left out so many key details, so much subtext, told so many half-truths that you'll never ever trust me again even if I laid my conscience bare. Even if I said I really wanted you to listen for once, I really had something to get off my chest, something you needed to know. Something that might help you begin to understand.

It's like they say, I guess. Never trust a three-hundred-pound white man with a mohawk. Never trust a writer, not the least of whom, a *mem-wha-ist*.

Just ask my mom, my dad who never molested me. Just ask my wife, all my friends I never talk to anymore. My aborted son, the rest of the kids that'll never have to call me dear old dad. All my many adoring fans.

It's just that I can be a real son of a bitch like that sometimes. But I guess that's just what comes with the territory, you know. What with me suddenly being this big-time writer and all.

Benjamin Drevlow

Acknowledgments

"A Good Ram is Hard to Find" originally appeared in *Fiction on the Web*; "Buried Treasure" originally appeared in *Fried Chicken and Coffee*; "How Much I Want You to Love Me" originally appeared in *Fiddleblack*; "Jonesing for Jesus" originally appeared in *Neat*; "My Childhood PTSD as Triggered by the Following Movie Montage" originally appeared in *Revolution John*; "So Much Love" originally appeared in *The Fiction Pool*; "Notes On Jumping" originally appeared in *Los Angeles Review of Los Angeles*; "The Weathermen" originally appeared in *Rock Bottom Journal*; "Work" originally appeared in *Working Stiff: The Anthology of Professional Wrestling Literature & Art*.

To Christina, all the clichés are clichés and yet they are all still true. You are everything. And I don't deserve you.

To Adam, goddamn, I don't know where I'd be as a writer if it weren't for your support. Couldn't ask for a better editor and friend.

To Sheldon Lee Compton. Your friendship and support keeps me going on the days where I think what the fuck's the point of any of it, anyway.

To Brian Alan Ellis, Chris Dennis, Alice Kaltman, David Tromblay, Tommy Dean, Devin Murphy, and Daren Dean for being nice enough to lend their names and kind words to this weird mother.

To Chad, Michael, Sexton, Stacie, Schumacher, Kat, Chris, Holly, Brian, Janine, Nick, Amy, Matt, Louisa, Todd, Caitlin, Elena, and David. My fam.

To family who have yet to disown me, despite the many many reasons.

Made in the USA
Middletown, DE
06 February 2022